What readers  The Glendale Novels

"Just finished The Glendale Series and loved it! I have never read a story that described the salvation experience so completely and beautifully! As a Christian and avid reader, I sometimes get nervous about starting a new book because I don't know if the content will line up with my faith and beliefs, but this was never an issue in these books. Thank you for writing books that Christians can enjoy! God Bless!!!"

– Julie B.

"I have read lots of Christian novels by top authors...but I find this series the best I have read. So well authored and covers situations that people are facing in today's world."

– Elaine P.

"So glad I found The Glendale Series. ...Your books have a bit of Kingsbury flavor and I haven't enjoyed a series like this since the Baxter Family books."

– Terri B.

"I discovered Ann Goering about a month ago. I have read every one of the books I could find on Amazon. I am 70 years old and wish I could have read Christian books like these when I was a teen. So many lessons in her books that take so long to learn."

– Linda S.

"Your books have been a blessing to me. So much examples and teaching, that we can get from your books for today's living. As for me, being God's minister will like to use your books in youth groups, women, family, etc... I pray that your books may be translated into other languages. I will like to have them in Spanish. Dios te bendiga Ann."

– Alida R.

"This was a beautiful story of the transformation of one young girl, a love story, and two young hearts. This is a refreshing book that is enjoyable as it does not have all the bad language and other things that many romance novels have. Give this a try, you'll be glad you did!"

– Mark Y.

"I am a lover of Karen Kingsbury, Terri Blackstock. I gave this author a try and got all 3 books on my kindle and have zoomed through them. Love them all. Wish she had more to read!"

– Lisa B.

"Glendale is such an inspiring book for teenagers. Every young person should read it. It made my walk with God stronger."

– Hayley

"From Glendale to Promising Forever, this series is worth sinking some time and serious prayer into. I read all three in a day and went back to read it again, slowly to savor the words and message. Wonderful series, fresh author!"

– Angie

"While the stories themselves were well thought out and conveyed, the spiritual side of the book was an inspiration. I read a lot of Christian romance and this series showed the strongest faith I have seen so far. Definitely brought me closer to my own faith and led me to very uplifting answers when I didn't even know I had questions."

– Vicki R.

"I recommend this for all parents and teens. Parents will gain a new perspective while teens will see their own version of the story in it."

– Shelby C.

"I really felt like I knew the characters. It was as if I could see them and their facial expressions and their movements. The author did a fantastic job of showing the power of love, emotional, physical and spiritual. I am so happy there are more books in this series."

– Liz M.

"At first I thought this was a good read for teens and planned to purchase a copy for my niece. However, as I continued reading, I fell in love with the characters. I was able to relate and identify in some way or another with all of them. Jessi, the main character who at first just got on my nerves with her behavior & attitude, captured my heart. Ann Goering really understands and portrays the hurt and damage that divorce and lack of relationship bring. I was reminded of Jesus' compassion, grace, and ravishing love for us!"

– D. Lopes

THE GLENDALE NOVELS

The Glendale Series

Mothers of Glendale

Ann
GOERING

PROMISING FOREVER
A Glendale Novel

COVERED PORCH PUBLISHING

Promising Forever

Copyright © 2011 by Ann Goering. All rights reserved.

Cover design copyright © 2011 by Ann Goering. All rights reserved.

Edited by Eileen Fronterhouse

ISBN-10: 0989086623
ISBN-13: 978-0-9890866-2-2

Library of Congress Control Number: 2013904215

www.coveredporchpublishing.com

www.anngoering.com

Requests for information should be addressed to:
Covered Porch Publishing, Ann Goering, PO Box 1827, Hollister, MO 65673

Printed in the United States of America

17 16 15 14 13 CofO 7 6 5 4 3 2 1

This book is dedicated to the Author of Life, the One whose way is always better;

My husband, who teaches me daily about the beauty of marriage and the true role and essence of a bridegroom;

And my sister, who has demonstrated lying down her life, wants and desires in selfless acts of love for the good of another over and over – I respect you so much for how you imitate Christ in this way, and as I have for the past two decades, continue to desperately need to learn from you!

One

"What colors are you thinking?" Jari Cordel asked, her hands clasped, her eyes shining. Jessica laughed. She had just returned from Glendale with Joe and the girls the night before after a wonderful Christmas with the Colby family. Today, the girls were at preschool, and Jari had begged Jessica to meet her for lunch. Jessica glanced down at the sparkly new engagement ring on her finger and again felt the unexplainable warmth spread through her. Her high school sweetheart, Joe Colby, had asked her to be his bride. Yes, a wedding was definitely in her near future, and Jari was obviously eager to begin planning.

"Well, we don't want to wait long, so—"

"Have you set a date?" Jari interrupted, on the edge of her seat, the chicken salad in front of her, forgotten. Jessi laughed again, her heart filling with appreciation for her step-mom.

Since the day Bill and Jari Cordel had picked Jessica up from the airport in Washington, D.C., Jari had been by Jessica's side every step of the way, loving her and supporting her in a role that fell somewhere between a best friend and a mother.

Jessica had stayed in her room for days, cold, empty and alone, mourning Glendale, Joe and all she had lost when she made the decision to set Joe free to follow his dreams and return to her father's house. Jari had been the one to continually reach out to her. When Jessica discovered she was pregnant with twins, Jari had been the one to go with her to every appointment, make sure she had the best prenatal care and rejoice in feeling the babies move. She helped decorate the nursery, think of names and prepare for their arrival. Jari had been with her the day she gave her life to Jesus Christ and had been a spiritual mentor every day since.

Jari had been with Jessica in the delivery room and stayed with her nearly every moment during those first several months, even getting up in the middle of the night to help Jessi get the girls fed and situated. She stayed at Jessi's side, carrying one of the baby carriers while Jessi carried the other, whenever they went out. She hovered over the young threesome, making sure they had everything they needed, and that Jessica was getting enough rest.

It was Jari who had homeschooled Jessica her senior year so she could get her high school diploma, despite being pregnant. She was the one who watched the girls day after day while Jessica took a heavy course load to graduate from college early. She had stayed up late to help Jessica study and cheered so loudly it was almost embarrassing when Jessica walked across the stage to accept her degree.

Jari had gone apartment hunting with Jessica and the girls, then furniture shopping. She helped them move in and get settled in their new apartment. Most recently, she watched the girls daily while Jessica worked, and sometimes even for weeks at a time when Jessi was called away to disaster scenes. Working in disaster relief demanded a schedule that wasn't conducive to being a single mom. Jessica never would have been able to balance a career and children if it hadn't been for Jari. And now she was helping her plan her wedding. A warm smile spread across Jessi's lips.

"We're thinking the second weekend in May."

Jari clapped her hands and let out a squeal. "Okay, that doesn't leave much time – four months – so we'll have to get to work. Have you decided on flowers or colors? Or a location? What about a guest list?"

"Okay, one question at a time," Jessica said, swallowing her bite of chicken sandwich, still smiling. "We thought about having the wedding in Glendale, because we both love it there, and we also thought about having it here in D.C., just for simplicity's sake. We haven't decided for sure yet."

Jari nodded. "That's understandable."

"I want it outside with a profusion of brightly colored flowers. Pinks and purples, oranges, lots of green," Jessi went on.

"Sounds beautiful," Jari agreed, nodding and forking in a bite of fresh spinach.

"We're thinking a small wedding, with just our families in attendance," Jessi finished. At this, Jari stopped chewing, which Jessica had expected. Jari was just starting to object when someone at the door caught her eye, and she glanced up, then smiled and waved. "Oh look! Your mom finally got here!"

The wedding conversation halted as Carla Cordel Martens rushed to the table. "So sorry I'm late! I was held up in court and then—! Well, I'm sure you read it all in my text."

"The important thing is that you made it," Jessica told her, standing up to give her mom a hug.

Carla hugged her back. "Good to see you, Baby Girl! How was your Christmas?"

"Wonderful!" Jessi answered.

"I'm sure...Christmas with the Colbys is always something special! How is everyone?" Carla asked fondly. "Oh, is that for me?" Carla continued, pointing to the shrimp salad they had ordered for her. Jessi nodded. "Perfect. Oh, and you even remembered to ask them to put the dressing on the side. Good girl." Carla flung her coat over the back of her chair and leaned over the table to quickly embrace Jari. "This was a great idea. Thanks for planning it, Jari."

"I had a feeling you were as eager to see your daughter as I was," Jari answered warmly.

As they all took their seats, Carla caught Jessica's left hand. "I'm still not used to seeing that on your hand."

"Me either. Sometimes it still surprises me," Jessica admitted, feeling a little sheepish.

"Good Lord, it is shiny!" Carla continued.

"And sparkly! The boy did good," Jari added.

Jessica smiled, looking at her ring and thinking of her fiancé. "Yes, he did."

"Anyway, how is everyone?" Carla asked, taking her first bite of salad. "Was everyone there? Kara, Kaitlynn and Kimberly?"

"Yes, and all their husbands and children! The family has definitely grown since the last time I was with the Colbys for Christmas," Jessi answered with a laugh. "The girls were so excited about having cousins. They had a ball! Carson and Samuel are older than the girls, but they all played together so well."

"And those are Kimberly and Greg's?" Jari asked, trying to put names together correctly. Carla and Jessi had lived next door to the Colby family during their year in Glendale, but Jari hadn't, and was just now trying to connect names and place children with parents.

"Yes," Jessica confirmed. "And they have Clinton, who's two, and Caiden who was born in November. Kaitlynn and Jake have Adam, who's three, and Austin, who was just born at the beginning of December. The girls were *enraptured* by the babies. They sat and cooed at them for hours."

"I bet they did," Carla answered smiling, getting a mental picture of her granddaughters with the new babies.

"And Kammy was feeling up to going back to preschool so soon?" Jari asked. Jessica waited until her mouth was empty before she answered.

"I guess. I was going to keep her with me today and just send Kels to school, but she insisted that she wanted to go and felt up for it. I think she misses her friends and just wants things to get back to normal. Her teacher promised to keep her in at recess, and that she would call if Kamryn started to look droopy. I haven't received a call, so I guess she's doing alright."

Jari shook her head in disbelief and gratitude. "What a miracle. Just a few short weeks ago, Kamryn was lying in the hospital, and we weren't sure she would ever wake up. If she did, doctors expected significant brain damage. Now, here she is back at preschool."

Jessica's eyes stung with sudden tears, and she tried to blink them away. It had been a miracle. An absolute miracle. Everything had turned out perfectly fine, but the memory of nearly losing Kamryn in a car accident was too fresh not to bring a few tears to her eyes. The memory of standing in the hospital room, not knowing if her daughter would live or die, made her stomach flop even now, even knowing the happy ending. She noticed that Jari and Carla's eyes were wet too, and she took a long drink of cold water. "It truly is amazing," she answered.

"Jess was just telling me what they're thinking as far as the wedding goes," Jari told Carla, changing the subject.

Carla turned to her daughter, clasping her hands in front of her in anticipation. "Ooo! What are your plans so far?" Jessica repeated what she had told Jari, finishing again with the fact that they wanted a small wedding.

"Why a small wedding?" Carla protested. "You're only going to have one – make it a party!"

Jessica shrugged. "It just isn't what we want. We already have the girls, and it's been such a process…. I think at this point we simply want the people with us who have walked the last seven years with us."

Jessica took a drink of water, unconcerned by the arguments Jari and her mom might have against a small wedding. She and Joe were solid on their decision. Between their year of dating in Glendale during high school, Jessica's decision to return to D.C., the girls being born, their five years apart, their 'coincidental' meeting on the street, Joe finding out about the girls only to walk out, and then the car accident that brought them all back together, it had been a long and intricate journey. No one could fully understand the meaning and importance of their wedding day except for those who had walked through the past several years with them. Only those closest to them could truly understand the joy their wedding would bring, and the story behind it all. Those were the people Joe and Jessi wanted to share their special day with – just their immediate families and a hand-ful of close friends.

"But Jess, what about all your friends? Your co-workers? What about Joe's friends? You know your dad is going to want to invite some of his friends and professional acquaintances. What about the church family? You're close to a lot of people. They'll be hurt if they aren't invited," Jari pointed out.

"And besides, Bill's in politics, and Joe was quite the star in college – news of your wedding will be leaked, and it will be big whether you want it to be or not," Carla added.

Jessica nodded. "We've thought of all of that, but we still want to keep it small."

Jari and Carla looked at each other as if deciding whether to keep pressing for a large wedding or give it up. Finally, Carla shrugged. "If small is what you want, small is what you will have." She squeezed Jessi's hand and smiled. "It's your day, and it's going to be exactly what *you* want."

"And what Joe wants," Jessi reminded.

"That's right," Jari agreed, her face still showing her disappointment. A large wedding would have been fun to plan, and Jessi knew that both her mom and step-mom had their hearts set on it.

"If you want small, I strongly recommend a destina-tion wedding," Carla continued.

"A destination wedding?" Jessi echoed. The idea had-n't even occurred to her while she was discussing wedding possibilities with Joe.

"Yes. For example, everyone you want at your wedding would fly to...the Bahamas and we would contract with a resort that would have everything set up. We could all enjoy the island for a few days, you two could get married on a beach with a sunset in the background, then we would all leave so you could have your honeymoon. If you want a small wedding, it may be your best option. A woman at my firm actually had a destination wedding about six months ago and raves about it. She said it was beautiful, special, they got great pictures, and it was stress and hassle-free."

Jessica tipped her delicate chin, considering the new option. She hadn't thought of a destination wedding. "And I could bring my own dress? And flowers?"

"Yes, you would bring your dress and any accessories. You could bring flowers if you wanted, or they could provide them. They'll cater the meal, make the cake, and decorate. Really, it sounds to me like you can be as involved as you want, or leave everything up to them. It's just what your preference is," Carla answered.

"Or, we could reserve the church," Jari offered, her face hopeful. "You could have the ceremony in the church and the reception outdoors with white tents, fine linens, white lights, swans, ice sculptures and a live band with lots of guests." Jari's expression was wistful. "It would be so fun to do all the planning and see it all take shape. It would be absolutely magical, Jess!"

Jessi smiled at her step-mom and reached across the table to pat her hand. "I know you want that for me, Jari, but this is what I want. Truly. I don't care about a big, fancy wedding. I just want to be married to Joe and be a family. Finally. It's been too many years coming. The wedding isn't as important to me as the marriage that will follow."

Understanding filled Jari's face, and she nodded. "Okay," she paused, and let a small smile slip. "But if you change your mind about the swans and ice sculptures, just let me know. I have the names of a few places here in town."

"And I know of an estate that would be perfect for the reception," Carla added. "Just in case you change your mind, know that we have you covered."

Jessica laughed. "If we do, you two will be the first to know." She directed her attention back to Carla. "I'll talk to Joe about a destination wedding. Thanks for sharing the option. Is it very expensive, do you know?"

Carla reached out and patted her daughter's hand. "You didn't grow up alone for nothing. I think after all the sacrifices Bill and I made to advance our careers, we can cover the cost of your wedding – be it destination or swans and ice sculptures. Whatever you want, it's yours." Carla pulled out her electronic calendar keeper. "Now when do we want to go wedding dress shopping?"

Jari and Jessi both rummaged in their purses to find their own calendars, and they compared free days until they found one that would work – a Sunday afternoon a week and a half away. "I think that will be good," Jari told Jessi and Carla. "We can go look several times if necessary, and there will still be time to make alterations or have a gown custom-made."

Jessi couldn't hold back a broad smile. She was going wedding dress shopping…for a wedding dress for herself! Six months ago, a wedding seemed to have no place in her future. Now, she had a beautiful engagement ring on her finger and was going wedding dress shopping with two of the most important women in her life.

"Can I invite Grandma, Hannah, and Kara to go dress shopping with us?" Jessica suddenly asked, realizing there were more women she wanted to include.

"Absolutely," Carla agreed, and Jari nodded.

"Okay. I'll make the phone calls tonight. I'm guessing Hannah and Kara won't be able to make it, but I'd like to invite them just the same."

"That's a good idea," Carla agreed and then with a wink, continued. "You have in-laws now. You can't leave them out!"

"Nor would I want to," Jessi added with a smile. Carla nodded in agreement.

"What's Joe doing today?" Jari asked, as if suddenly remembering that a groom came along with their wedding plans.

"He's at my house checking into schools to transfer to," Jessi answered.

Jari nodded past a drink of ice water. "Well, tell him we sure enjoy having him," she paused. "Not that we see him very much," she added, giving Jessi a teasing smile.

"We just got back," Jessi protested. "I'm sure he'll be around more this week."

"And then it's back to school?" Carla asked.

"Yes, although hopefully he'll be able to transfer to a school in or around D.C., so he'll be able to live close by in the months leading up to the wedding. If he's not able to transfer for the spring semester, he'll finish out the year in Michigan and transfer in time for the fall semester."

"Good! So you'll be sticking around?" Jari asked, obviously relieved.

"Absolutely. This is our home, and Joe thinks it's important to keep home the same in the midst of so much transition…especially for the girls."

"Smart man," Carla commented with a wink.

"Agreed," Jari added. "That way he can keep his wife, daughters, and in-laws all happy." Jessi laughed.

Hearing a familiar sound coming from her purse, Jessica pulled out her phone and turned off the alarm. "I have to run and pick up the girls from preschool," she told the others apologetically.

"Well, thanks for making the time to meet us for lunch. We've both been curious to hear how you're doing and what lies ahead," Jari said, standing up to give Jessica a hug.

"As if any of us ever truly know," Carla muttered under her breath as she snatched one of Jessi's untouched fries, before standing to give her daughter a hug as well.

"Absolutely! I was dying to talk to both of you in person! Okay, tell Dad and Tim hello from all of us, and I'll see you in a week and a half if not before." Jessi didn't miss Jari's crestfallen look. "Before, I'm sure," she added quickly.

"If you have to go into the office, or if you want to go on a date with Joe, bring the girls over! I'd be glad to have them!" Jari told her as Jessi grabbed her purse and picked up the ticket to see how much cash to leave. Carla took the receipt from between Jessi's fingers.

"I've got it, Hon."

"Thanks, Mom. I will, Jari! See you soon!" Jessi promised, heading toward the door.

Once in her SUV, her purse tossed on the seat beside her, Jessica thought over the lunch conversation. It was obvious that Jari had her heart set on a big, grand wedding – something out of a fairytale. Jessica hated to disappoint her, but knew that more than Jari wanted her to have a big wedding, she wanted her to have the wedding that *she* wanted. Jessi thought again of Carla's suggestion of a destination wedding and nodded to herself. It might be the perfect choice.

Once she pulled into a parking place in front of the preschool, she pushed her long, dark hair behind her shoulder and stepped out of the SUV, careful not to slip on the ice as she walked up the sidewalk. Why she chose to wear heels in January when there was a layer of ice and snow on the ground, she didn't know. She remembered standing in her closet that morning, trying to decide between warm and practical or foolish and cute. Sadly, the new black heels, dark jeans and short-sleeved black turtleneck with the silver chain belt looped around her hips had won. Thus, she slipped her way to the school door, shivering.

When she opened the front door, a warm burst of air greeted her, and she went to the front desk to sign the girls out. As she finished, she heard two shrill voices call out, "Mommy!" Kelsi came running to her, throwing herself around her legs as if she hadn't seen her for days. Jessica laughed and hoisted the dainty girl to her hip. "Mommy, Kammy and I got stickers. Mine is of a horse! See!"

Jessica looked at the sticker stuck to Kelsi's gray sweater and nodded. "It's beautiful!"

Settling Kelsi more securely on her hip, Jessi searched the room for Kamryn. She found her blonde-haired daughter sitting at a table with crayons, her broken leg stuck out to one side. Kammy waved at her, unable to come greet her as her sister had, and Jessi hurried to her. Setting Kelsi down on the floor, she hugged Kamryn and ooed and ahhed over her sticker as well.

"Whose sticker do you like better, Mommy?" Kelsi questioned, obviously convinced that Kamryn's puppy sticker was getting just a little too much of their mom's attention.

"I like them both," Jessica answered, lifting Kamryn gently, careful not to hurt her injured leg or casted arms.

"Yes, but whose do you like *better* – Kammy's puppy or my horse?" Jessica looked down at her spirited and sometimes bossy brunette.

"I like them both equally. It's not a competition, Kels. You both have very nice stickers."

Kelsi looked at the ground for a moment, then grabbed Kamryn's picture and held it up for Jessica to see as a way of making amends. "See Kammy's picture, Mommy? Isn't it pretty? She's drawing a rainbow."

"It's very lovely. I like all the purple."

"It's hard to draw with my casts on," Kamryn explained, her eyes downcast.

"Well, I think it looks beautiful," Jessica told her.

"Me too!" Kelsi agreed emphatically.

"Soon, both of you girls will get your casts off, and you will be able to draw, write, and play like you used to," Jessica continued.

She spent several minutes looking at what the girls had made at school, listening to their stories and talking to the teachers. She learned that Kamryn was quieter than normal at first, but Kelsi hadn't given her a chance to feel embarrassed about the casts she wore. Kelsi had drawn several of their friends around them and told the whole story of the car accident they had been involved in over Christmas break. She emphasized how brave Kamryn had been and how God had worked a miracle. After that, once the others stopped staring at her casts, Kamryn warmed up and started acting like herself again, the teacher said. Jessica smiled at Kelsi across the room. She might be a handful, but her heart was pure gold.

On their way home, Jessica listened to more stories and told the girls about her lunch with Jari and Grandma Carla. The girls were missing both women and gave them each a call on their way home to say hello and promise they would be over to see them soon. When Jessica finished the phone call to Jari, she realized how much it meant to her step-mom that the girls called, and how much the woman had missed all of them. Pulling into her parking place at her apartment building, she made a mental note to get together with Jari again soon, and make sure that her friend didn't feel replaced just because Joe was back on the scene.

Joe. He was standing out in the cold, waiting for her. Her heart skipped a beat, and a smile spread across her face. He was here. Waiting for her. Grinning at her. Waiting to help her carry in the groceries she had picked up before lunch, and unload the girls. He was waiting to give her a kiss and talk about how their mornings had gone. Waiting to spend the rest of the afternoon and evening together, just as they would for the rest of their lives. He was waiting for her, just as he had been for the last several years.

Two

"My mom came up with the idea of a destination wedding today," Jessica said as she drained the spaghetti noodles in a colander in the sink. She glanced at Joe to catch his reaction, and saw he was considering it while setting the table.

"Destination? As in…getting married in Florida?"

"Well, she mentioned the Bahamas, but yes, I suppose Florida would work. I guess you coordinate with a resort or hotel and they set up the whole thing. You simply bring the people and your clothes. Mom said it's a super simple, stress-free way to get married that is still beautiful and special. She knew someone who did it and loved it. She also said if we want to keep the wedding small, it might be our best option."

Joe nodded as he took in the information. He came back to the kitchen for forks. "Another benefit is that you can simply stay there for your honeymoon," Jessi continued. "After the ceremony, the guests head home and the couple stays. I asked about the cost, but Mom said they'll pay for everything. Besides, it surely wouldn't be any more expensive than a big, elaborate wedding here in D.C." Joe was quiet, processing. "What do you think?" Jessi finally asked, looking back over her shoulder to shoot a glance at him, curious about what was going through his mind. "Do you like the idea? Or would you rather get married in Glendale? Or D.C.?"

Joe turned, his green eyes meeting hers and she felt her heartbeat quicken. He stepped up behind her, forks and all, and held her for a moment, kissing the side of her face and then speaking close to her ear. "As long as you're marrying me, I don't care where we are…but a beach, the ocean, you in a white dress and an instant honeymoon sounds nice."

Jessica again felt butterflies in her stomach as she had so often during the past few weeks since Joe came back to town. She leaned back against him, tipping her head back to rest against his solid shoulder. "That does sound nice, doesn't it?"

"Mmhmm." He kissed her face again, and they both let the picture he had described soak in for a long moment. "And it would be fun to take a family vacation of sorts," Joe finally added. "I'm sure our family members would all enjoy it."

"Right. Not only would our families not have to worry about setting up or taking down decorations, making sure everyone is in the right place at the right time, and if the caterers know where to be and when, it would be a time when everyone could just relax and enjoy one another. The women could tan by the pool, the kids could build sandcastles, the men could golf. Our wedding would be like one big, week-long celebration – one without any stress, just relaxation and joy," Jessi agreed.

Joe smiled and brushed a kiss across Jessi's lips. "That sounds like fun." He stepped away after giving her a gentle squeeze, and continued to set the table. "It's definitely an interesting option. What do you think, Jess? Do you want to go away to get married, or have a wedding here or in Glendale?"

She took a moment to think before answering, wanting to make sure she was completely certain of what she was about to say. "I like the idea of a destination wedding."

Joe flashed her his characteristic grin. "So do I. A lot. Well, that settles it. We're going away to get married."

"Now we just have to decide where," Jessi reminded, stirring the tomato sauce and meatballs into the spaghetti noodles before dumping all of it out of the pot into her brilliant red pasta bowl.

"Let's get online tonight after we get the girls to bed and do some research on a destination," Joe suggested.

"Good plan." She caught a noodle that was hanging off the edge of the pasta bowl and popped it into her mouth.

"How was your day? Did you find out anything about transferring to a local seminary?" she asked. Joe finished pouring glasses of water before shaking his head.

"Nothing yet, but I still have a few places to check into that wouldn't be too far of a commute."

"But nothing here in the city?" Jessica asked, trying not to sound too disappointed.

Joe hesitated. "I'm having some trouble with credits transferring. If I transfer to any one of the schools I've checked into so far, I would have to start all over. The last year and a half would be wasted."

"So, if worst comes to worst, you just go back to Michigan, finish the year out there, and then transfer in the fall, right? Your credits would transfer after you complete this year?" Splitting up until May would be difficult, no doubt, but they could do it if they absolutely had to.

Joe shrugged. "Not according to what I was told today. I may have to finish in Michigan. But…like I said, I have more checking to do."

"So, what would you do if it's like that everywhere? Surely you're not thinking we would all move to Michigan. You don't want to wait another year or two to get married, do you? Would you just start all over here?"

Joe crossed his arms and made a face. "I don't know. That's something we need to talk about."

Jessi felt as if the picture she had formed in her mind of what their lives would be like after the wedding was crashing down around her. What was Joe saying? Would he actually ask her and the girls to move? Surely he wouldn't expect them to leave D.C. And she couldn't wait another year to marry him. The thought itself was heartbreaking.

She wanted him with her – needed him with her. She wanted him as her husband, and the girls desperately needed their father. "Isn't that what we're doing?" she questioned, defensive.

"Jess, it's not worth getting upset about yet," Joe answered, his voice reassuring. "Let me do some more calling tomorrow and see what I can find out. After I've covered all the bases, then we can talk about it and make an informed decision. There's no sense in jumping to conclusions or trying to make plans before knowing all of our options."

Jessica felt her shoulders slump. "You're right. I'm sorry. I just…I thought we decided to stay in D.C."

"That's still the plan. Don't worry. There are just a few complications, and we need to work through them."

Jessi felt herself prickle. A *few* complications? What else had come up? Was Joe having second thoughts about getting married? She took a deep breath and pushed away the troubling doubts. He likely hadn't meant it like it sounded. It wasn't fair to him to jump to conclusions. While Joe searched in her refrigerator for the parmesan cheese, she put the bowl of pasta and the tossed salad on the table and went to find the girls.

She found them in their bedroom playing with their dolls. Kamryn was awkwardly brushing her doll's hair, her play inhibited by her casts, while Kelsi was taking hers for a ride in the baby buggy. Jessi stood in the doorway for several moments, enjoying the chance to watch them play. They were so engrossed in their play that they didn't notice her standing there. Finally, she interrupted them.

"Girls, time to eat. Are you hungry?"

"What are we having?" Kelsi asked instantly, seeming rather suspicious. Jessica smiled.

"Spaghetti and a salad."

"Yum! I love spaghetti!" Kamryn said, her eyes lighting up.

"Me too! It's my favorite, Mommy!" Kelsi chimed in,

already running toward the kitchen. Jessica couldn't help smiling as she bent to scoop up the nearly immobile Kamryn. As if she didn't know her daughters loved spaghetti – that was, after all, why she had chosen to make it.

Kelsi raced to the table and was up in her chair, her fork in hand, by the time Jessica and Kamryn reached the dining room. "Slow down, Little Miss. Everyone has to be seated at the table, and we have to pray before you can eat," Jessica reminded, getting Kammy situated.

"I know, I know! I'm just getting ready!" Joe and Jessi laughed at Kelsi's enthusiasm and Jessi headed into the kitchen to get salad dressing out of the fridge.

"Oh, I already have them, Jess," Joe told her, motioning to the table.

"I know, I just don't see the Italian...it's been my favorite lately," she explained, grabbing the dressing in question out of the refrigerator door.

"Oh. Well, I'll make sure to grab it next time," he replied cheerfully. She flashed him a smile, then followed him to the table to sit down.

They all joined hands as Joe prayed, thanking God for the day, for their family and for the food before them. As soon as he was done, Kelsi had her plate lifted for her helping of spaghetti. Joe was ready to oblige and put a scoop on her plate when Jessi abruptly stopped him. "She can't be served first. Kels, you know the rules. Kammy, hold your plate up, please."

Kelsi turned puppy-dog eyes up to Joe. "I just really love spaghetti, Daddy." Jessi watched as Joe's expression changed from confusion to pure adoration and felt a twinge of annoyance. He was not going to be much help in disciplining if the girls only had to look sad and call him 'daddy' to make his heart melt.

Jessica stood, seeing that Kamryn's casted arms were growing tired from holding her plate out. She took the pasta spoon from Joe and scooped Kamryn's pasta, then used the salad tongs to fill her salad bowl half full, adding dressing to her salad and parmesan cheese to her spaghetti. Joe reached toward Kelsi's plate, drawing a grin from the pouting girl, and Jessi glanced up. "Joe, she has to be served last." Her tone was snappier than she meant for it to be.

Joe watched Kelsi's grin fade back into a pout and averted the spoonful of pasta to Jessica's plate instead. "Why does she have to be served last?" Joe asked, putting obvious effort into sounding casual.

Jessi shot him a pointed look, then looked to her dark-haired daughter. "Tell him the rule, Kels."

"Those who want to be first have to be last. Jesus says if you want to be first in the Kingdom of heaven, you must become last," Kelsi told him obediently. Understanding showed on Joe's face, and he nodded.

"That's right. He does say something like that." Joe glanced at Jessica, a grin filling his face. "It's a good rule." He finished dishing up Jessica's plate and his own and then, when everyone else had their food, he served Kelsi.

A few moments of silence passed as everyone enjoyed the meal. Kamryn reached for her cup, and after taking a drink, made a face. "What is that? Water?" she asked in disbelief.

Jessi glanced at the glasses. "Oh, I guess it is."

"But we *always* have milk with spaghetti," Kamryn and Kelsi said together. Joe looked from one daughter to the other.

"I'm sorry, girls, I didn't know," he told them, his face falling. Jessica shot Joe an apologetic look as she stood and collected the girls' cups.

"I'm sorry, I should have told you, I just didn't think about it. Some things are just second-nature." She dumped out the girls' water and came back with cups of milk. As soon as she set them down, both girls took big drinks of the creamy white liquid. Jessica took her seat, reached over and squeezed Joe's arm. "I'm sorry. I should have told you. It's just what we always do – we always have milk with spaghetti."

"Just like you always have Italian dressing." Regret filled Joe's face as soon as the testy comment came out. He reached out for Jessi's hand. "I get it, Jess, really I do. I've been gone a long time. You three have your own traditions and ways of doing things. And I'll learn them, I will. It's just going to take some time."

"And we can make new ones," she offered. "We can be flexible, can't we girls?" His words, combined with the look on his face, made Jessi's heart sad. The last thing she wanted was for Joe to feel like an outsider in their family. Both girls nodded. "I'll try to do a better job of explaining things and filling you in," Jessi told him, meeting his pale green eyes. His smile warmed her heart.

"We'll help, too!" Kelsi promised.

"After spaghetti, we each have three Oreos that we dunk in our leftover milk. When we have pizza we always get to split a can of soda, and we always have movie night and pizza night on the same night," Kamryn told him, her green eyes sincere.

"When we have tacos, it's Mexican night and we always get to wear our sombreros and say 'gracias' instead of 'thank you'," Kelsi added.

Joe grinned at the girls. "That sounds like a blast." Both girls nodded, their mouths full of spaghetti noodles once again. He turned to Jessica. "I like that you do theme nights. How fun."

"It *is* fun," Jessica answered, her eyes sparkling. "Especially Mexican night. These two make beautiful senoritas!" The girls giggled.

After they all finished their spaghetti, Joe rummaged through the cupboards until he found the package of Oreos and put three by each plate. They ate their cookies, finished their milk, and he cleaned up dinner while Jessica and the girls laid out Candy Land. They sat around the table, talking and laughing as they played the game together. Kelsi made it to the castle first and got up and did an adorably funny victory dance that made the rest of the family laugh. Then, it was one last trip to the potty and off to bed, where the four of them piled onto Kamryn's bed for a bedtime story. Joe read the book of Kelsi's choosing, since she was the winner of the game. Prayer came next, followed by goodnight hugs and kisses. Joe turned the light out after Jessica flipped on their pink nightlight.

Out in the hall, Jessica pulled Joe into a hug, letting her forehead rest against his firm shoulder for a long time. The air around them felt comfortable and sweet. "You don't know how nice it is to have you here...to do that together," she told him. He tipped her chin up so he could see her delicate face and rubbed his thumb back and forth along her jaw. "I've spent almost five years doing that alone, wondering what it would be like if you were here, reading the bedtime story, leading the prayer... Now that you are, it feels so right," she finished, her voice thick with emotion.

He gazed down into her face for a long moment, and then kissed her gently. "Let's go find a place to get married and set a date. I don't want to leave every night for much longer. I want to be here with you, have an evening with you, go to bed together, wake up together, eat breakfast together... I don't want to say goodbye anymore. I want to spend all of our days together...I want to live life together."

Jessica smiled. "I want that, too." She did. More than anything. She allowed him to lead her to the living room by her hand. "You know, Mom and Jari were trying to convince me today that we need some big, elaborate wedding with all of our friends, family, and acquaintances, but I don't care about any of it," Jessica said as Joe sat in the computer chair and drew her down onto his lap. "You know why?"

"Why?" he asked, looking up at her, his expression a mixture of adoration and amusement.

"Because I just want you. You're the one and only thing I want to get out of our wedding." He smiled and pulled her close, kissing her.

"Is that right?"

"Yes," she barely whispered, overcome with emotion. It was true in every way. She had wanted Joe Colby since the first day she met him in a 7-Eleven in the small town of Glendale. She had wanted him when he refused to date any girl, much less her. She had wanted him when they started going out – wanted all of him, all the time. When she had left Glendale for the purpose of setting him free to chase his dreams of a college football career and becoming a pastor, she spent over five years wanting him, wishing he was with her. Now, with his ring on her finger and Joe sitting in her house, she wanted him – wanted him as her husband, wanted him with her every day for the rest of their lives. She wanted to wake up with him, go to sleep with him, raise their children with him, grow old with him. "Yes, that's right," she finished. He grinned at her.

"Well then, let's find ourselves a place to get married."

Joe let her run the mouse while he typed, and they found site after site of establishments that hosted destination weddings. They could get married in a castle in Europe, a mountain lodge in Colorado, or a palm-covered hut in the Caribbean. They weighed the pros and cons of each general location and decided that although mountainous regions were beautiful, and Europe charming, they wanted to go someplace warm. They wanted to go where there was an ocean and a beach, where their family could hang out in hammocks or go snorkeling, and where they could later enjoy the same activities on their honeymoon. Concentrating their search, they continued, determined to find a location before the night was over.

"Get married on our white sand beaches with the vivid Caribbean Sea as the backdrop," Jessi read. "After the ceremony, walk down the beach with your guests to white tents strung with lights, complete with chandeliers and china, to celebrate your union in style. With sand beneath your feet and the option to have the tents open to reveal the sea, your guests will be treated to one of three exquisite menu options while enjoying the ultimate island experience."

Joe ran his eyes down the page. "Hammocks, snorkeling, scuba diving, wind surfing, tennis courts, a four-star golf course, all inclusive dining packages, three pools, a spa, great reviews…it looks like this place has it all."

"And look at the pictures…it's beautiful!" Jessi breathed.

Joe grinned. "I think we just found our destination. Would you like to marry me in St. Lucia?"

Jessi grinned back. "Yes, please."

Three

Joe stood to meet Jessica as she walked in the door of the coffee shop. He saw men at several tables notice her arrival. He couldn't blame them. His fiancé was absolutely stunning. He gave a little wave to get her attention, and then watched as she sent him a warm smile and made her way through the crowded shop to join him at his table.

He hadn't seen her at all the day before as he had been busy trying to find a seminary to transfer to before the semester started, and then process what he had learned. He was grateful she had been willing to forfeit an hour of sleep to meet him before she went to work. Now, he felt himself filling with dread as he remembered what he needed to tell her.

Upon reaching him, the dark-haired beauty wrapped her arms around him and gave him a sweet kiss. She looked up at him out of crystal blue eyes and said, "I missed you yesterday." Looking down into her pretty face, he couldn't help stealing another kiss.

"I missed you, too." He held her for a long moment, then reluctantly released her. They didn't have much time before she had to leave. He motioned for her to sit down and handed her the large vanilla latte he had ordered for her. He took his own mocha in hand and sat in the chair facing her. He studied her face for a moment, then took a drink of coffee, leaned forward and took her hand in his.

"Just tell me. What's wrong?" she asked, appearing to be bracing. He inwardly chided himself for worrying her. He forgot how well she knew him. Of course she would have heard it in his voice last night when he called. She had probably been worried about it all night. He should have just gone over to her house, no matter how much he needed time to process and plan.

"I can't change schools. My credits won't transfer. I would be starting all over. My years...my work...my school loans would all be wasted." She looked disappointed and relieved, all at the same time. He understood her disappointment but not her relief.

"Is that all? It's just for a semester. You can move after you finish out your year in Michigan and start school here in the fall. It will be hard for sure, but we'll get through it. It's not ideal, but we've been apart for almost six years... a few more months isn't the end of the world. We'll just make it work." He could tell she was trying to be brave. That made him hesitate to tell her the rest, but he knew he had no choice.

"I can't transfer at all. Nothing changes after this semester."

"What do you mean?" Her voice was dull.

"I mean, my credits won't transfer after I finish out the year any more than they'll transfer now. It's something about my school's accreditation. It's just as legit after I graduate, but the credits won't transfer before graduation."

Jessica sat quietly for a moment, and he watched an array of emotions play across her face. Shock, disappointment, confusion, uncertainty and fear were all there. She wet her lips. "So, what does that mean?"

"Well...it means we're going to have to rethink our plan."

"Rethink which part?" She sounded scared.

"I want to marry you, Jess, more than anything in the world," Joe quickly assured her, knowing she was getting the wrong idea. He saw the relief flash across her face and knew his assumption had been correct. How could she doubt that?

"So...what? We push the wedding back for a year or two?"

The very thought was almost unbearable. He had already missed out on almost six years with his family. He wasn't going to let that continue for even another year or two. "No. I won't push it back."

"Then you'll start completely over here? At a seminary in D.C.?"

"Jess, I can't. I would *waste* a year and a half. Do you know what kind of money pastors make? We're already going to be paying off my student loans for several years. I can't stand the thought of racking up any more debt than necessary, especially when we would be paying for something I've already done and paid for once."

"So, what are you suggesting?" He could see that she genuinely didn't see any other option.

"After the wedding...come to Michigan with me." There. He had said it. He watched the surprise fill her beautiful face.

"You want the girls and me to move to Michigan? Joe, I thought you said the girls needed the stability of staying here."

"That would be ideal, yes, but this is the best option we have, Jess...at least the best option I can think of."

She hesitated. "I don't know. That's a lot of change in their little world."

He had known the hesitancy would come, yet it crushed him. "Is transition a greater disadvantage than being seven before they have a father?"

"I didn't mean that," Jessica started, but Joe held up his hand, knowing he was responding out of hurt, being quick to make assumptions.

"I know that's not what you meant, Jess, but I'm afraid those are the options. Either we can wait to get married for a year or two, and I can visit a couple of weekends per semester, or we can get married in St. Lucia the first week of May as planned, and you and the girls can move to Michigan to be with me while I finish school."

Joe hesitated for a moment before scooting his chair closer to hers. He framed her face with his hands. "I want to marry you, Jessica Cordel. I've wanted to since high school. If there was any way for me to move here to be with you while I finish school, I would, but I can't. I've tried. I've exhausted every option. I want it as much as you do, but there's just no way to make it happen. It's either you and the girls move to Michigan to be with me, or we have to wait to get married. I've waited over half a decade...I don't want to wait any longer. I don't think I can." Jessica bit her lip and looked away. His heart fell. "Do you want to wait, Love?" he questioned. She shook her head.

"It's just a lot for the girls," she finally said. *And you,* he thought, but he wisely didn't put voice to it.

"I know it is, but we'll all be together – we'll be a family."

Jessica pulled away, shaking her head. "I know, and that's wonderful, truly, but you don't understand. In the last few months they've gotten new grandparents, new aunts, uncles, and cousins, a *father*, been in a car accident, and are still on the mend. They have to share my attention with someone else for the first time in their lives...and now we're going to move them to Michigan? Joe, I want to be married, too, and if it were just me, I would say absolutely, but part of being a parent is protecting your children and doing what's best for them...I just don't know about moving them right now."

Joe was able to hold his tongue for only a moment. "A part of being a parent that I don't understand because I'm not one...is that what you mean, Jess?" Her eyes flashed at his accusation, and she simply shrugged. He felt hurt explode through him, making a hundred comebacks come to mind.

He wanted to remind her that the only reason he hadn't been an active parent for the past five years was because he didn't know about his children, whom she had kept a *se-*

cret from him. He wanted to throw it back in her face. Instead, he took a deep breath and eased back in his chair. They sat silently for several long moments.

"Well, Jess, here's what I think," he finally started. "I think those little girls deserve a family. A real, complete family with a mommy *and* a daddy. I think they're resilient and strong. I think if we turn moving into a happy adventure, they'll be happy. They're kids. They'll adapt. They'll do great. They're fighters, Jess – I witnessed that firsthand in the hospital. But they fight best when we're all together, right? That's why we brought Kammy in to be with Kels – so we could all be together. They're going to be okay, you're going to be okay, in D.C., in Michigan, it doesn't matter. What's important is that our family is together. That's what I think is best for them. And maybe I haven't been in their life for as long as you, but I love them so much and I want to protect them and do what's best for them, too. Right now, I think that's being together as a family."

Joe watched the fight go out of his fiancé, and she reached for his hand. "You're right. You are. It doesn't matter where we live as long as we're all together." Joe held her eyes.

"Are you sure?" he asked.

She nodded. "Yes. I want to be with you. I want the girls to be with you. I want all of us to be together. So, if you're going to be in Michigan, then…we'll be in Michigan, too. I'll have everything packed by the wedding so when we get back from the honeymoon, we can pick up Kels and Kam, load our belongings in a truck and move to Michigan." Warmth flooded Joe as she spoke.

"You are a strong, brave woman, Jessica Cordel, and I love you so much," he told her, genuinely meaning every word. He brushed the hair out of her eyes and she caught his hand and held it against her face, leaning into it.

"I don't want to be away from you this semester," she told him, her pretty face turning down into a pout that made her look every bit as cute as their four-year-olds. He kissed the tip of her nose.

"I don't want to be away from you either."

"When do you have to leave?" she asked.

"School starts Monday."

"So soon?" she almost wailed. He couldn't help a grin. After all those years of thinking she didn't want him, it felt good to be wanted.

"At least we know that in four short months, we'll be married and on our honeymoon," he reminded.

Jessi held his eyes for a moment, her smile slow but spreading. "That's a nice thought."

He laughed. "Yes, it is."

His mood turned serious again, and he rubbed a strand of her dark, silky hair between his thumb and forefinger. "Love, I know I haven't been with the girls as long as you have. I know I didn't watch them grow up, or see them take their first steps or...or attend even one birthday party yet. But I promise that I love them, and I will love them for the rest of my life, just as I love you and always will. I know you've had to be the strong one, the leader, the protector for the last five years, but I promise you, Jess, I will lead this family and be the rock that stays steady when everything else is wavering. I promise I will protect you and the girls and make every decision from this day forward with you, and them, and our family in mind." He touched her face tenderly. "The weight doesn't rest solely on your shoulders anymore. You no longer have to do this alone."

Jessica's lip trembled, and Joe reached out and drew her into his arms, resting his face against the side of her head. She always tried to be so strong, but the weight of leading their family was never one she was meant to bear. She was strong and resilient and brave, but it was never meant to be her responsibility. He could see she had felt the weight of it acutely. It had taken a toll. Knowing that made his heart hurt.

He felt her relax against him. "I've waited a long time for that…for you to say that. I don't want to be alone or to do this alone anymore."

"I know that I'm leaving in a few days, and you will be living life alone again for the next four months, but I will only be a phone call away. Let's do it together long distance. I'll fly back for a couple of weekends and the girls' birthday, and maybe you can come west and visit me once or twice, too."

"Absolutely." She took a drink of her latte, and smiled up at him. "I can't wait for May." Joe brushed the hair back out of her eyes, his heart full, and grinned at her.

"Neither can I, Jess. Neither can I." A few minutes later, he watched her walk away from him, headed for the door so that she could make it to work on time. He wished they could spend the rest of the day together. Unfortunately, though, her life couldn't be put on hold just because he was in town.

His mind racing ahead, he thought again of how difficult it would be to leave on Saturday. Boarding a plane that would take him hundreds of miles away from Jessica and the girls was the last thing he wanted to do. After nearly six years of being apart, he knew he didn't want to live like that for even another day; especially not now. Not when marriage was within sight. Not when he knew he was a father. Not when the girl of his dreams, the girl who had captured his heart in high school, was waiting for him. It would likely be the longest four months of his life. Thankfully, on the other side of those four months was a flight to the Caribbean, a warm vacation with the people he loved most in the world, a sandy ceremony, a long-awaited honeymoon, and Jessica. Then they would come back for the girls, move to Michigan and begin their life together.

Joe pushed himself to his feet, a smile on his face, and headed for the door after throwing away his empty cup. He would go back to Bill and Jari's, pick up the girls as planned, and have a father/daughter day while Jessica was at work. He would finish out their day with a trip to the movie store and a stop at a pizza place. After Jessi got off work, he would experience one of Jessi and the girls' movie nights. It was going to be a fantastic day.

~~~~~

Had she really agreed to move to Michigan in just a few short months? Jessica twirled a capped ballpoint pen through her dark curls and contemplated the newest turn in the journey she was on with Joe. The past six months had been a blur.

Last year, life had finally evened out, and for the first time in a long time, she felt like she could really settle in, build a life and get comfortable. She had finished high school, finished college, and had a job she loved. The girls were in preschool, the three of them had their own apartment and were building a life for themselves in D.C. Then, Jessi bumped into her high school friend, Tacy, in her favorite coffee shop downtown. It had been a blast from her past that had caught her completely off guard. For the first time in five years, her year in Glendale had collided with her life in D.C.

A month later, she was stopped in her tracks when Joe called her name on a crowded D.C. sidewalk. He had appeared seemingly out of nowhere, just a chance meeting in the middle of one of the most unlikely places. They went to dinner and parted as friends. She was confident that was how their chance meeting would end, and that was how she wanted it, even if she was lonely. But then, Joe showed up on her doorstep with roses and coffee the next morning, and the girls answered the door. In an instant, he knew the secret she had kept from him for the past five years. He turned, walked away, and she didn't hear from him again for months.

She thought her collisions with Glendale were finally over until she stepped out of the elevator with the girls only to find Hannah and Kara, Joe's mother and sister, waiting at their front door. Next, was the car accident – the drug-impaired thief who ran from the police only to slam into her SUV, nearly taking her daughter's life. Within hours, Joe was at the hospital. They were waiting for news together, and he held her while she cried. He met the girls, prayed over Kamryn, and slept in the hospital chair. Jessi lost her heart to him all over again.

On Christmas Eve he had asked her to marry him, and she said yes. Together, they returned to Glendale with Kelsi and Kamryn. For the first time in five and a half years, she drove by the ice cream shop where they used to get ice cream, and saw the high school they had both attended. They stayed at his parents' house, took walks through the forest they had explored together as teenagers, and sat against the old oak Joe called his 'Jesus tree'. Some part of her that had been missing since she left Glendale to return to D.C., came to life again, and she realized that she no longer simply loved the boy from her memories, but she was very much in love with the man Joe Colby.

Now, they were back in D.C., in her home, planning their wedding and making plans for her to pack up the girls and their life in order to move across the country in a few short months. She had never even been to Michigan. She didn't know what it was like. She didn't know if they would live in the city or in the country, if there were trees, or if it was flat and barren. She didn't know if there would be a preschool for the girls to attend or a place to have her hair cut, but none of it mattered. Because, as crazy as the last six months had been, as many times as she had been completely taken off guard, scared to death, weeping to the point of barely being able to breathe or so full of joy that she felt as if she were coming apart at the seams; regardless of whether moving to Michigan felt like too much right now, one thing stood out among all the rest. She was in love with Joe Colby, and in four short months, she would be his wife.

"What are you smiling about, Miss Cordel?" Jessica startled, dropping her pen. Recovering, she smiled at her co-worker who was looking over the top of the cubicle wall they shared.

"I'm just happy I guess."

"It wouldn't have anything to do with that handsome fiancé of yours, would it?" Beth asked, gesturing toward the picture of Joe, Jessi and the girls that had been taken at Christmastime and was now proudly displayed on her desk.

Jessica couldn't hold back another smile. "It has everything to do with him."

"Oh boy. You're smitten. It's a bad case of it, too," Beth joked as if it were a fatal illness. Jessica laughed.

"Yes it is – a real bad case. And I'm fairly certain that it's completely and entirely incurable."

~~~~~

"Girls, before we eat pizza or watch the movie, we're going to have a family meeting," Joe announced, sitting down on the coffee table so he could face his daughters. Jessica sat down on the couch and pulled Kammy onto her lap, cuddling the little girl close. Kelsi looped her arm through Jessica's, watching Joe intently.

"A family meeting? What's that?" Kelsi asked, her dainty face screwed up in confusion.

"It's something we're going to start having if we have something very important to discuss that involves the whole family," Joe explained.

Kelsi sat up a little straighter, obviously pleased to be included in an important discussion. Kamryn simply sat and watched him, her pixie-like face open and curious, her eyes kind and gentle.

Joe glanced up at Jessica and caught her eye. She smiled at him and nodded for him to continue. He returned her smile before averting his attention back to the girls. He had been planning this family meeting all day. "First, we'll always pray together. That's how we'll end it too." Joe took

Kelsi and Kamryn's hands, and Jessi did the same. "A family that prays together stays together," he explained, quoting something he had heard his parents say time and time again. They all bowed their heads, and Joe led them in prayer. When he looked up, he had four curious green eyes, just like his own, looking at him expectantly. "Girls, you know that I go to school, right?" he started.

"To semimeminary," Kamryn answered, nodding, oblivious to her mispronunciation of the word.

Kelsi nodded as well. "To be a pastor and learn about God."

"That's right," Joe answered. "But I go to school in Michigan which is a long ways away...even longer than how long it took to get to Grandpa and Grandma's for Christmas." The two pairs of green eyes grew big.

"That's a very long way," Kelsi whispered to Kamryn.

"I was going to switch schools, so I could go to school here in D.C."

"Even though Mommy and Daddy aren't getting married until May, he wanted to live close to us so he could see you girls every day," Jessi explained.

"Right. But after I made a lot of phone calls, I learned that I can't start school here unless I take all the classes that I've already taken in Michigan, over again. That would take a very long time, and I would be in school even longer. Does that make sense so far?" Both girls nodded. Joe took a deep breath. "So, on Saturday, I have to leave to go back to Michigan. We'll do something fun during the day, then you and Mommy will take me to the airport. We'll say goodbye, and I'll get on a plane to fly back to school."

"For how long?" Kamryn asked, worry showing on her sweet face.

"Just until May," Joe answered, holding her gaze. "But I'll be back for your birthday, spring break, and hopefully one other weekend before then. At least one weekend this spring, you girls and Mommy will get on a plane and fly to Michigan to see me."

"How far away is May?" Kamryn asked, tilting her head.

"Four months," Joe answered.

"How long is four months?" Kelsi asked Jessica.

Jessica smiled. "Four months ago you girls were just starting preschool after summer break. Do you remember when you started back to preschool in the fall?"

Kelsi's eyes grew wide. "That's a very long time for you to be away."

Joe nodded. "Yes, it is."

"What happens after the four months?" Kelsi continued, crossing her legs and leaning forward, looking very much like a lady. "Will you come back?"

Joe glanced at Jessica again, and she smiled at him for a few long moments as if giving him permission to say what needed to be said next. "Well, you girls and me and Mommy, and all of your grandpas and grandmas, aunts, uncles, and cousins will fly to an island—"

"What's an island?" Kamryn interrupted.

"It's a piece of land surrounded by water. In this case, it will be very warm and have lots of palm trees and sandy beaches."

"Can we make sandcastles?" Kamryn asked, her eyes shining. Joe and Jessica laughed.

"Yes, you girls can make all the sandcastles you want," Jessica answered, hugging Kammy close.

"On the island we – Mommy and I – are going to get married. Then we'll be a family. A real family. That means I'll get to live with you guys then!"

"In the same house?" Kelsi questioned, her excitement evident.

"Yes! In the same house."

"Woohoo!" Kelsi jumped down off the couch and did a victory dance similar to the one she had performed after winning Candy Land, and Kammy clapped her hands and cheered as best she could, considering her casts.

"After we get married and we all become a real family, we're going to pack up all of your things, and you're going to move to Michigan to live with me while I go to school next year."

"We're going to move? Like when we moved from Grandpa and Jari's to our apartment?" Kelsi questioned.

"Yes. Just like that, only it's going to be far away," Jessi answered.

"Will Grandpa and Jari and Grandma and Tim and GG Maybelle come too?" Kamryn asked.

Jessica shook her head. "No. They will stay here. This is their home."

"But this is our home, and we're moving," Kamryn said, confused.

"Well, Kam, when you become a family, your home is where your family is. Our home is going to be where Daddy is."

Jessica's answer seemed to satisfy both girls. "So... how do you feel about that?" Joe asked, unsure about what to say next.

"Will we be able to take our dollies?" Kamryn asked.

"Of course," he answered.

"Our beds?" Kelsi questioned.

"Absolutely," Joe told her.

"Our goldfish, Henry?" Kamryn asked.

"We wouldn't think of leaving him behind." Joe braced, waiting for whatever Kelsi was about to ask – she had a scheming look on her lovely young face.

"I think this all sounds very good, *if*—" She let the word hang.

"If what?" Jessica asked, shooting Joe an amused look.

"*If* we can get a puppy when we get to Michigan."

"Well, aren't you a little opportunist," Joe observed, reaching out to tickle Kelsi. She giggled as she kicked and squirmed to get away. Kamryn exchanged a look with her sister, then looked from Jessica to Joe expectantly.

"Well? Can we get a puppy when we move to Michigan?" she asked.

"Daddy and I will discuss it," Jessica answered, giving both girls an amused smile. Again, the girls seemed pleased with her answer.

"Any other questions?" Joe offered.

"Can Kels and I wear dresses when you get married?" Kamryn questioned.

"Without a doubt," Jessi assured her.

"And throw flowers?" Kamryn continued.

Joe looked at his daughters' shining faces. "You want to be the flower girls? Is that what you're saying?"

"Precisely," Kelsi answered for her sister. Joe grinned as he grabbed Kelsi, tossed her lightly in the air, caught her, and then flopped down on the couch beside Jessi and Kamryn. Kelsi giggled as he settled her on his lap.

"You girls will be the prettiest flower girls ever," he answered. Kelsi wrapped her arms around Joe's neck and brushed her nose against his, then grinned at him.

"Mommy calls those Eskimo kisses."

Joe smiled at her, his heart brimming. "Well, I like those Eskimo kisses very much." Kelsi squeezed his neck with her small arms, then sat down in his lap, leaning back against his chest.

"Let's pray," Joe suggested. He motioned for Jessica to lead them in prayer. She thanked the LORD for the girls, for Joe, for their family, for family meetings and for the move that was in their future. She prayed for the details to come together and for peace for all of them. Joe echoed her 'amen'.

"Pizza time!" Joe announced, and Kelsi jumped off the couch and was in the kitchen in a flash. "Stay here. I'll bring everything in," Joe told Jessi as he stood. She smiled up at him and snuggled down in the couch, getting comfortable with Kamryn. He stopped in front of her and bent down to rub his nose against his fiancé's. "I hear you call these Eskimo kisses."

Jessi laughed lightly. "Yes, sir."

"What do you call these?" he asked before kissing her soundly on the lips. She gently pushed him back, laughing.

"I call those trouble." Joe grinned.

"Trouble?"

"Yes, because I like them too much." Kamryn giggled in Jessica's lap, and Joe tousled her hair, then glanced back up at Jessica. She was watching him with so much affection shining in her eyes that it took his breath away.

"Daddy! Come help me! I can't carry the soda *and* the pizza!" Kelsi declared, pulling the box of pizza from the kitchen counter. Joe jogged into the kitchen just in time to catch the box before it fell on the floor. He helped Kelsi get a good grip on it and sent her and the pizza into her mother. He grabbed glasses and three cans of soda – one for him, one for Jessica, and one for the girls to split, just as he had been instructed on spaghetti night.

Four

Jessica tipped her head and studied Joe over the candlelight. He was stunningly handsome – the kind of guy that made women stop and stare. He could have been an actor in Hollywood, stealing the hearts of women everywhere. He could have been a professional quarterback, basking in fame and glory, women and money. But the humble man in front of her wanted nothing more than to be a pastor, get married to his one and only girlfriend, and be a father to his daughters. He was most comfortable in a t-shirt and jeans and didn't seem to notice his looks or the fact that others did. But Jessica noticed.

She noticed how his pale green eyes seemed to pop against the ever-tanned hue of his skin, the way his rich brown hair fell across his brow, the sturdy and masculine line of his jaw and the way his defined muscles showed even under his suit jacket. He was still the most handsome man she had ever seen…and he was hers. It was difficult to comprehend.

He must have felt her attention. He glanced up at her. She was almost sure he blushed, but he didn't look away. With a ring on her finger and strict physical boundaries in place to guarantee they stayed far away from what their relationship had resorted to almost six years before, a little flirting seemed harmless.

"You are a very attractive man, Joe Colby," Jessica told him, her eyes dancing.

"You are the attractive one," he contradicted, clearly embarrassed. His face softened. "Your beauty is unmatched by any other." Sincerity shone in his green eyes, his gaze was intense.

She fumbled for words, feeling shy after the way he had turned her compliment around. "I'm glad you like my dress. I hoped you would."

"It's not your dress that makes you beautiful." She felt heat rush into her cheeks at the intensity in his voice. She glanced away.

"Sometimes, I think about all the girls that must have chased you over the years and I feel....a little insecure," she admitted. She had always felt a little unnerved by the beautiful, blonde Heather Crebel, who had been after Joe all through high school, and she knew Heather was only one of many. Jessica felt her mind drifting to what college must have been like for him, wondering if there were any girls of a similar mind at his seminary. A lot could happen in four months.

"Don't!" Joe's emphatic response startled her. He leaned forward and reached for both of her hands. "Know that I am being one hundred percent truthful when I say that your beauty is unmatched by any other. I have never seen a girl that compares to you. You are the definition of beauty, Jess, the absolute definition. There has never been, and never will be, a girl who turns my head like you do or who makes me feel the way you make me feel." He sent her a charming grin. "Trust me. There is *no* need for you to give room to insecurity. Know that I am captivated by you, by your beauty." Jessica felt the blush returning. She pushed her salad around on her plate for a distraction and finally took a bite. He did likewise, and she felt her embarrassment subsiding.

"They love you, you know," she said after several seconds of silence, watching him again.

"Who's that?" he asked.

"Kamryn and Kelsi. They are ecstatic to have you in their lives. They told me yesterday morning that you are everything they ever wanted in a dad...and that you're even funny, too." Joe laughed, but then his expression grew serious. He cleared his throat and reached across for Jessi's hand again. She watched him, confused.

"Jess, Honey, thank you for telling me that. It means so much to me," he started. She could sense the 'but', and watched him closely, curious as to what would come next. "But tonight, I only want to hear if you love me. I love the girls so much, but tonight I want to go on a date with my fiancé. Just you and me. Tonight is a night for romance... I'm not looking at you and seeing the mother of my children. I'm looking at you seeing the girl who has me stumbling over my words, hoping you'll glance my way, and making my knees shake." He quirked a smile at her. "Tonight I wish we could sit in my truck and make-out like we did in high school."

Jessica felt warmth spreading through her even as color poured into her cheeks. Their relationship was so different than it had been in high school. It was now based more on conversation and true relationship than physical attraction and chemistry as it had been, yet that part of it was still there, running strong under the surface.

She focused on the message he was trying to convey rather than his ending statement. She knew Joe loved the girls, knew he meant nothing by his statement other than to let her know he loved her for who she was, not simply because she was the mother of his children, or because he felt obligated to marry her now that he knew about the girls. He wanted to marry her because he loved her. *Her.* Jessica Cordel. The spoiled rich girl from D.C. who was nothing like the girl he had pictured and yet the only girl he wanted. His words were like water to her dry and thirsty heart.

"I asked my parents once what made their marriage last and how they are more in love today than when I was young," Joe continued, "and they said that when they went out on a date, they really went out on a date. They didn't talk about us kids. They didn't refer to each other as Mom or Dad. They didn't talk about laundry, who was going to take who where, or which one of us might need braces and if they could afford it. My dad said he has dated Hannah Colby for over thirty years. I want that."

Jessica tilted her head as she pictured going through the coming years with that in mind. "I want that, too. It sounds nice to focus on each other when we go out."

Joe grinned. "Or stay in."

Jessica laughed. "Yes, or stay in," she conceded.

"Let's set aside time every week to spend quality time as a couple and a separate time to meet as parents," Joe suggested after another bite of salad. "We can schedule a day to get up early and share a cup of coffee while we discuss school, braces, schedules and discipline, but let's also set aside time to come together as man and woman, husband and wife, only. I am marrying you, Jessica Cordel, not our daughters. Even though I love that they are part of the package and wouldn't have it any other way, I want you all to myself for at least a little while every week. If I can have that, then I think I can share you with the kids for the rest of the week." He winked at her, letting her know that although he was very serious, there was humor laced in his words.

Jessica knew her eyes were shining at him again. Her smile was so big she likely looked cheesy, but she didn't care. The picture he painted was beautiful. The idea of having Joe all to herself, like it had been in high school, like it had been in August when they went out for dinner, like it was now, was incredibly appealing. "I think I can live with that."

He grinned. "Good." The waiter swooped in to take the salad plates they had just emptied. Only seconds later, he returned with their main course.

"Tell me how you're feeling about the wedding. What still needs to be done? What can I help you with from Michigan? Who do you want to invite?" he paused. "Jess, if we do a destination wedding, will you truly be happy with it? Will you ever wish we had a big, traditional wedding here in D.C.? Please tell me the truth."

Jessica swallowed her first bite of her entrée while watching Joe in amazement. He was still as thoughtful, attentive and involved as he was in high school. He cared about what she cared about and found ways to get involved, even in things that most guys shirked away from. He wanted to be involved in her life, her thoughts, and her activities as much as she wanted him to be. It was amazing and she appreciated it immensely.

"Truthfully, I think a destination wedding sounds perfect. It's what I want. I want our family there, I want pictures to hang on our walls, I want to wear a white dress, and I want you. That's what matters to me."

"You're sure?" he pressed.

"Completely," she answered without hesitating.

"Okay. Then that's what we'll do. So, what's the next step?"

"Wedding dress shopping," Jessi answered, her eyes shining with excitement.

"That's right. Is Mom going to be able to make it?"

"Hopefully! She was checking flights last I heard. Mom, Jari, and Grandma are all planning on it. Kara and Justin are in Colorado skiing this weekend, or else she would have come."

"You're going Sunday?"

"Yes. After church."

"Good. I'm glad you have something to look forward to this weekend," Joe said, only referring to his looming departure in passing. It was something neither of them wanted to think about, especially not tonight. "Will you send me a picture in the one you choose?"

Jessi made a face at his question, which had been accompanied by a grin. "Absolutely not. You can see it at the ceremony and not before."

He was still grinning. "Deal. Okay, what else needs done?"

"Well, I sent Mom and Jari the link to the resort, so they're taking care of arrangements on that end. I think the next thing we need to do is write up a guest list, pick invitations, and send them out."

"Good thinking. Let's work up a list tonight when we get home. It'll be mostly family and a few close friends?"

"Right. At least that's what I would prefer," Jessi answered.

"Me too," Joe agreed.

"What about attendants? Do we want any? If so, how many groomsmen do you want?" Jessi questioned, moving down the running checklist she had in her mind.

~~~~~

Jessica tried not to cry as she watched Kamryn cling to Joe as they neared the point in the airport where they would have to say goodbye. The girls wanted to walk him to his plane, but Jessica had explained they couldn't because of security. They didn't understand.

Going to the aquarium earlier had seemed like a good idea at the time – a way to have one last afternoon of fun together before Joe had to return to Michigan. However, Jessica now realized it had left the girls tired as it had disrupted naptime, which would do nothing to help with goodbye.

Kamryn clung to Joe, her face buried in his shoulder. Kelsi, who was settled on Jessica's hip, was already crying unashamedly. It was going to be a long night. Jessi was glad it was already seven o'clock. By the time they said goodbye, she put the girls in the car and they drove home, it would be bedtime. Her daughters could get some sleep, and she could deal with the sorrow and loneliness Joe's absence would bring, without having to be strong and upbeat for them. Over the last several weeks, she had gotten used to having him around. Being all alone again was going to be a difficult adjustment.

They reached security, and it was time to say goodbye.

"Don't go, Daddy! Please don't go!" Kamryn wailed against Joe's neck. Jessica felt tears sting her eyes. She noticed that Joe's were watery, too. She stepped close and put her hand on Kamryn's back, trying to help. As she did, Kelsi reached out and latched on to Joe as well, hanging from arms that were now wrapped tightly around his neck. He dropped his duffel bag in order to hold on to her. Jessica bit her lip. She looked up at Joe, and knew he didn't know how to say goodbye when all he wanted to do was stay. Her heart filled with compassion. She took a deep breath and then smiled. This was what she was trained to do; she helped people say goodbye and move forward. At least this time it was only for a few months.

"Girls, Daddy has to go. If he doesn't go, he's going to be late for school. Miss Mandy wouldn't like it if you were late for school, would she?" The girls shook their heads, still pressed against Joe's shoulder. "Well, Daddy's teachers wouldn't like it either. He would get in trouble. Do you want Daddy to get in trouble?" Another shake of the heads. "You know, girls, in just a few weeks we'll come pick Daddy up in this exact same place. We'll get all dressed up, drive to the airport, and stand here to wait for him. He'll come through that door right there, and you can run and hug him to say hello. How does that sound?"

"I wish you were coming home today, Daddy," Kelsi told him, sniffing.

"Me too," Joe answered softly. Jessi smiled as she looked up into his pale green eyes and saw how much he was struggling with having to leave. Although she didn't like to see him sad, it felt good to see how much he loved them.

"Right, but if he doesn't leave, then we won't get to have the excitement of seeing him come back! It will go fast, you'll see. Remember how Mommy has to leave a lot for work? But you have so much fun at Grandpa and Jari's, and we talk on the phone and see each other when we video chat, and I'm back before you know it, right?" Two little nods. "Well, it will be the same way with Daddy. And before he comes back, we can spend a whole day baking him yummy treats. We can make cookies, and—"

"Pink cupcakes with pink frosting?" Kelsi asked, her face brightening in anticipation.

"Mmm! That sounds delicious. My tummy will be growling from now until I get back, just waiting for those pink cupcakes," Joe responded, sending a wink to Jessica.

"And I can make a sign with your name on it for Mommy to hold up so you can see where we are," Kamryn offered.

Joe nodded. "That would be great, Sweetie."

"Those are great ideas! So, let's tell him goodbye now so he gets back that much sooner!" Jessica wondered for a moment if there would be more tears and clinging, but instead, the girls gave their dad little girl hugs and sweet little kisses. They told him they loved him and how much they would miss him. He promised he would call every night before bed.

Then, he held each girl off to a side, and Jessica stepped close, taking her turn to give him a hug and a kiss. Her eyes met his, and she smiled, knowing her eyes were teary again. She might be able to help the girls say goodbye, but her tactics didn't work so well on herself. "I wish it were May," she admitted.

"It will be soon," Joe told her, kissing her. "I love you." His voice was full of emotion, and she smiled.

"I love you, too." She held her hand against the side of his face and smiled up into his eyes for just a moment. "I love you so much, Joe Colby." She stepped back, knowing this time of dread and expectation, wanting to keep him but knowing he had to leave, was going to be the worst. After he left, they would simply be counting down the days until they saw him again. That would be better. The second goodbye would be easier, and the third easier still, knowing that

May was getting ever closer. They just had to get through this one.

Joe handed her Kamryn first, after giving the little girl one last squeeze. He let her get situated on Jessi's hip before setting Kelsi on the ground and guiding her hand to Jessica's. With both girls detached, he bent to pick up his laptop case and duffel bag. Then, he stepped forward to kiss Jessica one more time and shot them all a grin.

"I have the three most beautiful girls in the entire world." Kelsi and Kamryn giggled. "I'll be back soon," he promised, as he started walking backward. "And I'll call as soon as my plane lands to let you know I made it safely."

A stab of fear shot through Jessica. What if his plane crashed? What if this was goodbye? What if she never saw him again? What if the wedding in May, date nights every week, growing old together...what if all of it never happened? What if he never called and she never saw him again? Taking a deep breath, she pushed the fear away. He had to get on the plane. He had to fly back to Michigan. There was no way around it, and thus, fear was not going to help anything. She had to let him go, be strong for the girls, and trust that her fiancé was in God's hands, as he had been his entire life. She was confident that He knew best. She propped up what she hoped was a convincing smile.

"I love you!" Joe told them one last time, addressing them all.

"Love you!" Jessica, Kelsi and Kamryn answered in unison. Then he turned to get in line to go through security. Instead of standing to watch him weave back and forth through the crawling line, prolonging the goodbye, Jessica turned toward the exit, pulling Kelsi along with her.

"So, girls, what kind of cookies should we make him? Maybe we can even make him some this week and send a care package through the mail. That way he can eat our yummy cookies at school. Do you think he would like that? But we can't tell him – it will be a surprise!"

By the time Jessica drove across town to their apartment building and pulled into her parking place, both girls were sound asleep. She got them unbuckled and prepared herself for the long walk to the door, through the building, the ride up the elevator, the walk down the hall, unlocking the door and getting the girls to bed, all by herself. She felt weary just thinking about it. She had been spoiled over the last month by having Joe around. Going back to being a single mom was going to be rough.

"Looks like you could use a hand!" She whirled at the familiar voice behind her, and threw her arms around her dad. Of all the times she had not wanted to come home to an empty house and face toting her two sleeping daughters in to bed by herself, this had to top the list. And now, her dad was here to help. He patted her back gruffly. "We thought you might want a little company tonight," he told her when she stepped back. Jessica glanced at the glass door of the building and saw Jari wave. Jessi waved back.

"You were absolutely right," she told him, feeling close to tears. She was so thankful for her family.

Bill lifted Kelsi, who didn't even flinch, and went around to get Kammy while Jessica shut the door of the SUV and grabbed her purse out of the front. Once both girls were out of the vehicle and sleeping on their grandpa, Jessi locked the doors and hurried to follow him inside, out of the cold January night air. "What are you feeding these girls?" Bill asked, repositioning the limp little sleepers. Jessi laughed.

"They're heavy, aren't they?" Bill grunted his agreement.

Inside, Jari gave her a long hug, then looped her arm through Jessica's as they made their way to the elevator and up to Jessi's apartment. Bill helped her put the girls to bed, and Jari made tea. Once the girls were sleeping again, the three of them sat in the living room, drinking their hot tea while talking. They talked about the wedding, Joe, the events of the past month, a bill that was before the Senate, and the plans for wedding dress shopping the next day. After church and lunch, Bill would take the girls home for their naps, and Jari, Jessica, Carla and Maybelle would swing by the airport to pick up Hannah before heading to the bridal stores.

Jessica's cell phone rang. After confirming it was Joe on the caller ID, she answered and chatted with him for several minutes. His plane had landed safely. He was in a taxi and almost home. They hung up when he reached his apartment, and Jessica hung up happy. He was safe, and they were only weeks away from seeing each other again.

She joined back in the conversation going on around her and it flowed pleasantly from subject to subject until it was late and everyone was yawning. Once Bill and Jari left, Jessica went to bed and found that she wasn't as miserable as she had expected to be. After all, it was only a few weeks before Joe would be back for the girls' birthday. And it had been really nice to have her dad and Jari around to fill the silence and keep her company on a night when she had expected to feel utterly alone. It had been a very thoughtful act on their part, and Jessica reminded herself to thank Jari again when she saw her in the morning.

Her cell phone beeped and Jessica grabbed it from the nightstand. It was a text message from Joe. A simple 'I love you.' She went to sleep smiling.

Five

"We're going wedding dress shopping!" Jari sang, dancing around in the driver's seat as she navigated through Washington, D.C. traffic.

"We will if we make it," Carla added under her breath. "Jari keep your eyes on the road and stop dancing. If you want to dance, pull over and let me drive." Jessica laughed, both at Jari's excitement and Carla's motherly instruction. They had the whole crew – Carla, Maybelle and Hannah were in the backseat of Jari's SUV, and they were on their way to the first bridal shop.

"Sorry. I'm just so excited! We're going wedding dress shopping!" Jari said again.

Carla finally smiled. "Yes, we are."

"It's about time!" Hannah added, her smile broad.

"It sure is," Maybelle agreed, reaching up to squeeze Jessi's shoulder. Jessica looked back to smile warmly at her grandma.

"Jessica, fill Hannah and Mom in on where you've decided to get married," Carla ordered, all business as she flipped through a bridal magazine looking for styles to get them started once they reached the store.

"You've picked a place?" Hannah asked, leaning forward for the story.

"Yes, but it just happened," Jessica explained. "We decided to have a destination wedding in St. Lucia. We'll all fly to the island, stay at a resort, and simply enjoy ourselves for six days. Then, we'll have the ceremony Friday evening on the beach, hopefully at sunset, followed by a reception dinner. After the wedding, Joe and I will stay in St. Lucia for our honeymoon."

"St. Lucia? A wedding on the beach? Jessi, that sounds beautiful!" Hannah gushed, clapping her hands. Jessica turned around to describe the setting, growing excited once again about the place where she and Joe would marry.

"There are white sand beaches, clear blue waters, hammocks, pools and snorkeling. There's absolutely everything any of us could want to do on a vacation! The ceremony will be all set up for us so there will be no stress and no hassle – it will simply be a time for celebration! After the ceremony, we'll walk down the beach to white tents that are open to the ocean, and there will be chandeliers, fine china, and white linen tablecloths."

"And did I tell you they can do an ice sculpture?" Jari interjected, addressing Jessica. Jessi grinned and looked back at Hannah.

"And I guess there will be an ice sculpture."

"It sounds beautiful...and perfect," Hannah agreed, her eyes shining. "It sounds absolutely breathtaking and elegant while still being a great way to keep the crowd small."

"That's exactly what I said," Carla threw in.

"I'm sure it will make for some beautiful wedding pictures, Dear," Maybelle added.

"Yes it will! I can't wait to see them. Oh," Jessica paused and turned to Jari, "we need to make sure they arrange for a photographer."

"I'm sure they do, but let's check. Put it on the list," Jari agreed. Jessica pulled out the notebook Jari used to keep track of things she wanted to ask the resort about, and added the photographer.

"I know you want a small wedding, but I also know there are a lot of people who will want to attend. Maybe you should think about sending out wedding announcements with a wedding picture after you get home, so people can get a glimpse of the ceremony," Hannah suggested from the backseat. Jessica considered the option.

"I like that. It would show people why they weren't

invited. We'll make sure it's an island shot. It would let them know we thought of them and do value them. I like it."

"And maybe, if you want to, you could have receptions in D.C. and Glendale so friends and extended family members could congratulate you in person. You could have a slideshow with wedding pictures," Hannah continued. "One of Kara's friends from college was married in her husband's hometown last year. A week or two later she had a little reception where she grew up so friends and relatives could celebrate with them, even if they couldn't make the trip."

"I think that's a great idea," Jari added. "I've been to several receptions like that."

"Me too," Carla added. "It wouldn't have to be huge or super elaborate, Jess, but might be a nice way to include people who you're close to, but not close enough with to invite to St. Lucia."

"Yeah, that is a great idea. I'll talk to Joe about it," Jessi promised.

"We're here!" Jari exclaimed, pulling into the parking lot of an upscale bridal store. Jessica looked at the dresses in the windows and couldn't believe that they were about to walk into a bridal store and look for a wedding dress for *her*. It seemed surreal.

Jari parked, and the five women got out of the SUV and walked in, chattering away. Carla walked with Jessica, and showed her some of the dresses she had marked in the magazine. Jessica picked five that she liked. Inside, after connecting with Suzanne (the consultant they had an appointment with), Carla showed Suzanne the dresses Jessi liked in the magazine.

"She's going to have a destination wedding, so we would like something suitable for a wedding on the beach. These are some styles she might like, but feel free to show us any other dresses you think she should see," Carla said, taking charge. "You're the expert."

The woman flipped back and forth between the pages, then looked up at Jessica through black-rimmed glasses that sat low on her nose. "An island wedding?"

"Yes."

"What month?"

"May."

"May...it's a good month for a wedding." Tucking her black hair behind her ear, she wrote down Jessica's measurements, then showed them back to a private dressing area. She instructed Jessica to wait in the changing room and the others to have a seat in the plush chairs the sat around a large mirrored area with a pedestal Jessica would stand up on in her dresses. There were lights and mirrors everywhere, and Jessi felt both overwhelmed and in awe as she realized that all of the lights, the mirrors, the dresses, were for her. This time, she wasn't a bridesmaid shopping for a wedding dress for a friend – she was finally the bride! And the most important women in her life were sitting around for the single purpose of oohing and aahing, and helping her choose the perfect dress. Her heart swelled with love and appreciation for each of them.

Suzanne came back with several dresses draped over her arm. "I have a dress that is similar to each of the styles you identified, though custom-made and much classier. Each of these dresses is handmade and specially designed. You will not find the same dress in any other store, and no other bride will have worn it." Suzanne's voice was laced with pride as she ran her hand delicately over the yards of white fabric. "They were each uniquely designed by me and my design team. With that said, don't feel the least bit bad if you don't like one or all of them. We have many dresses, and we want to find the one that is perfect for you – the one that will make you feel like the most beautiful woman in the world. Now come, let's get started."

Suzanne hung the dresses in Jessica's room, shut the velvet curtain and prepared the corset and undergarments while Jessica undressed. While Suzanne worked on fastening the long line of hooks and eyes on the corset, Jessica looked over the dresses. "There are six here," she said in surprise. "I only showed you five styles that I like."

"I brought the five styles you like, and I brought the dress you will get married in," Suzanne answered, giving her a knowing look. "Now stop looking at them and stand still. Let me put them on you, and you can look at them in the mirror. Every dress is its best when it's on the person it was made for."

"Will you tell me which dress is the one you think I'll choose?" Jessi asked, feeling like a child on Christmas morning.

"No. You will choose first, then I'll tell you if it's the one I think was made for you," the small woman answered firmly.

Suzanne prepared the first dress and helped Jessica into it, spending several minutes lacing it up correctly. The laces that made the dress fit like a glove on Jessica's slender frame were on the inside of the dress as the back was rather plain. Jessi craned her neck to see the back and what Suzanne was doing, but was mildly scolded and told to face forward. There was no mirror in the room, and Suzanne was lacing the bodice up so tight and jerking so hard on the laces, that Jessica didn't even get a glimpse of the dress as she was busy bracing herself. Still, it felt wonderful on, and the fabric was smooth and delicate under her hands.

"How's it going in there?" Jari asked from her chair.

"We're almost done. Be patient, Sister! You can't rush art." Suzanne called, her lips pursed.

"Oh, she um, she isn't my sister," Jessica tried to explain to Suzanne quietly, embarrassed for Jari. A hush had fallen over the four women who were waiting.

"No? Isn't the dark-haired lady your mama and the blonde your sister?" Suzanne asked, not knowing how insulting her vocalized assumptions would be. Jessica felt her cheeks flame, hoping that neither her mom nor Jari had heard, but knowing they both had.

"The dark-haired one is my mother, but Jari, the blonde, is my step-mom," Jessica explained as quietly as she could.

Suzanne's eyebrows shot up. "Oh. My mistake."

Jessica was no longer in a hurry for Suzanne to finish; she was dreading having to face her mom. To be wedding dress shopping for her daughter with the woman her ex-husband had an affair with, had to be a little hurtful on some level. To have it assumed that woman was your daughter had to add injury to insult, despite the fact that Jari and Carla were now, by the grace of God, on good terms.

"I would gladly claim her though," Carla called out, getting in on the conversation going on in the dressing room. The four women waiting laughed, the tension dissipating and merriment returning. Jessica let out a breath of relief. She was grateful her mom had reacted so kindly, and made a mental note to thank her later.

"You're done. Go out and show off how beautiful you are," Suzanne said, sweeping back the curtain. Jessica had yet to see the dress she was wearing, but as she walked out, the four women's mouths fell open in admiration.

"It's beautiful, Baby Girl," Carla said, her eyes uncharacteristically moist as she came forward to help Jessica step up onto the pedestal and turn toward the mirror.

Getting her first glance of the dress, Jessi's eyes grew wide. "Wow," she breathed softly, running her hands over the skirt.

"Absolutely beautiful," Carla finished.

"Yes, it is," Jari agreed solemnly from behind her. Hannah was dabbing at her eyes with a tissue. Maybelle was all smiles.

Jessica let her eyes run over every detail of the dress. The fabric was satin and shimmery, just barely off-white. It was a modern, one-shoulder dress, with the only strap going around her upper right arm. The pleated strap added a slightly slanted top edge to the dress, as it extended across her chest and wrapped snuggly around her left side. The bodice was also pleated and slightly slanted, drawing attention to the dropped waist where a large satin flower became the focal point. The a-line skirt was simple and smooth. The dress was simple enough for an outdoor wedding, slightly dramatic and sophisticated-looking with the one-shoulder design, and beautiful enough that the four women behind her had tears in their eyes.

Suzanne stepped up on the pedestal with accessories. "See, you think about pulling your hair over like this," she pulled Jessica's long dark hair into a low ponytail on the left side and pinned in a large satin flower that matched the one on Jessi's hip perfectly, "and wearing jewelry like this. This is what I thought of when I was designing this dress. But if you don't like it, you do what you want. It's your day." She secured a single strand of pearls around Jessica's left wrist and another strand around her neck. Upon closer inspection, Jessica noted that the satin flowers were adorned with small pearls, as well. "Will you wear a veil?" Suzanne asked. Jessica shook her head no, still staring at her reflection.

She looked like a bride. The dress, the jewelry, the flower in her hair, it was all perfect. She ran her hands over the skirt, over the pleated bodice, over the fabric that formed the neckline.

"Well, what do you think?" The dark-haired dressmaker was smiling a knowing smile.

Jessica noted that the women behind her were holding their breath. She looked at Suzanne and smiled. "I love it. It's perfect!" Maybelle clapped her hands, and Jari bounded off her seat and was instantly beside Jessica, inspecting the dress and the flower in her hair.

"It *is* perfect, Jess! It is! I love it! You look beautiful. This dress is just...it's you! All over. It's so elegant! It's simple enough for a beach wedding, yet absolutely stunning!"

"I know!" Jessi bubbled, clapping her hands in delight. "I didn't really know how to describe what I wanted but—" Jessica stopped midsentence. Carla was standing behind them, obviously hesitant to join her daughter with Jari there. Jari noticed at the same time. "This is it," Jessi finished softly.

"You need to try on some shoes with it," Jari declared. "Suzanne, can you show Hannah and me your shoe selection? We'll pick out a few pairs, Jess, and be back." Suzanne agreed and led Jari and Hannah away.

Jessica turned. "Well, Mom, what do you think?" In what the years had proven to be a rare coincidence, Carla had tears in her eyes. Jessica hoped it was because of how she looked, and not because she had discussed the dress with Jari first. When Carla's face blossomed into a smile, Jessica knew her mom's tears were simply those of a mother realizing her daughter had grown up.

"I think it's absolutely *beautiful*," Carla answered, drawing her slender fingertips below her eyes.

Maybelle was standing with them now, her arm around Carla's waist, her face radiating joy and admiration. "That it is. This is the dress, Jessi!"

"Do you think I need to try on the others?" Jessica asked, swaying back and forth in her dress. She loved the feel of it under her hands and how it felt when she swayed. She felt like a princess. She felt like a bride – something that, in years past, she thought she would never be.

"Only if you want to, but I don't see any need. You seem absolutely sure about this one," Carla answered, drying her tears. She stepped forward to straighten Jessi's skirt and readjust the pearl necklace.

"As sure as you are about the groom," Maybelle added, still smiling.

Jessica grinned. "I am. I don't want to try on the rest!"

"Then don't. There's no need if you know you already

found your wedding dress," Carla agreed.

"Your mother speaks from experience. Remember how the first dress you tried on was the perfect one, too, Carla?"

Carla laughed. "Yes, I guess it was. Guess we have something else in common," Carla told her daughter, bumping her with her hip. As she looked at Jessica's reflection in the mirror, the woman's face grew thoughtful. "I was as sure about William Cordel as you are about Joe. I was so in love with him."

"You sure were. There was no changing your mind," Maybelle agreed, coming up on Jessica's other side to smooth out the shoulder strap of Jessi's dress.

"I was beyond confident that he was the man for me, that I loved him and that we would live happily ever after."

"You were?" Jessica asked, surprised. She had never heard her mom talk about the beginning of her relationship with Bill. She had never heard about it when it had been good. Now, she felt something like the rumblings before an earthquake in her heart and didn't know why.

"Absolutely. He was a good guy back then...before politics changed him."

"He was always a bit smug and power-happy for my taste," Maybelle interjected quietly.

Jessica turned to Carla. "You really loved Dad before you got married?"

Carla laughed. "What kind of a question is that? Of course I did! Do you think people ever start out hating each other? If they did, why would they ever get married? No, he was charming, sweet and handsome, and I was in love."

"She was just as ecstatic as you are the day *we* went wedding dress shopping," Maybelle told Jessica, smiling at the memory. Jessica smiled, too, tucking the tender moment with her mom and grandma away to think about later, squelching the uneasy feeling it had created in the pit of her stomach.

"Enough about that," Carla said, waving the memory away with her hand. "Look at you. You're going to be a bride! You're getting married! You're going to get married in this dress, Baby Girl! On a beach, with the ocean behind you, to the man you've loved for so many years! In *this* dress!"

Excitement came flooding back, and Jessica turned back to the mirror. "I am, aren't I? In just four months!" She clapped her hands, giving a little shriek of happiness. The next four months could not go fast enough.

"Jess, Honey, look at these shoes we found! Aren't they perfect?" Hannah exclaimed, coming back into the room, holding out a pair of off-white heels. The heels were thick, and only an inch high. The thin straps that held them on, one across the foot and one that circled the ankle, were so thin they didn't even show under the small pearls that lined them. The pearls were the same color and size as the ones on Jessi's jewelry. "The heel is perfect for an outdoor wedding – it's thick enough that it won't constantly be sinking in the sand, and look – they're the same pearls! Isn't that fantastic?" Hannah continued.

Jessica took the shoes. "Wow! They really are perfect! Look, Mom, Grandma," Jessica held the shoes out to show the others. Maybelle fingered the pearls.

"I've always thought pearls were classy. I might even like them better than diamonds." Maybelle's comment drew loud opinions from the others in the room as they all weighed in.

"Come on, try them on. I'll help you," Jari told Jessica, kneeling down in front of her. Jessica lifted a bare foot and Jari strapped the shoe on, then they did the same with her other foot. "Perfect!" Jari told her, standing up and dusting off the knees of her slacks.

"So, you are ready to try on the others?" Suzanne asked, giving Jessica a knowing look.

"I think I'm done, Suzanne. This is the dress I want to

get married in," Jessi answered, unable to stop smiling.

"You're sure? We still have five more. You might want to try them on, just to be certain. You don't ever want to look back and wonder."

Jessica looked around the room at the women she loved to get their opinions, starting with her mom. "Unless you want to, you don't need to look any further, Baby Girl. That's your dress."

Maybelle nodded. "You aren't going to find a dress more beautiful or more perfect for you."

"I love it, Honey. But if you need to look at more so you're sure, this is the time to do it," Hannah counseled. Jessica nodded, thinking it over. Hannah made a good point.

Jessi looked at Jari, and Jari was beaming again…or still. Jessica wasn't sure which. "It's your choice. You could try on a hundred and come back to this one or simply choose it now."

Jessica laughed. "It's true. I'm going to choose this one in the end. I already know it. Suzanne, I don't want to try on any more dresses. I choose this one."

Suzanne smiled her knowing smile. "Okay, then stand still and let me figure out if I need to alter it. Are these the shoes you're going to wear, or do you want to look around?"

Jessica shook her head, holding her dress up and lifting a dainty shoe-clad foot. "These are perfect."

The small woman pulled out a pin cushion full of pins, knelt at Jessica's feet and began to measure, fold, and pin, marking how high to hem the skirt. "I want it to just brush the top of your feet since you're getting married in the sand. You don't want a dirty dress at the reception."

Happy conversation filled the room as the women around Jessica began chatting – chatting with one another, with Suzanne, and with the woman who came to help Suzanne pin the dress. Jessica listened to the happy hum for a few moments, then redirected her gaze to the mirror.

She was getting married. She was wearing her wedding dress. Her mom, step-mom, grandmother and future mother-in-law had all taken time out of their busy lives to share this moment with her. They all loved the dress, the shoes, the accessories. She was wearing her wedding dress. She was getting married. She was marrying Joe Colby.

"Look at how she's smiling," she heard Jari whisper behind her to Hannah.

"How could she not? She is absolutely breathtaking and preparing to marry the boy she's loved since high school – the boy she thought she would never have," Hannah whispered back, dabbing at her eyes again. Jessica heard, but could not get the smile off her face. They were right. Simply by the grace of God, they were absolutely right.

Six

"What about this one?" Jari asked, holding up a knee-length, peach dress. Jessica turned and considered it. They had been looking for a bridesmaid dress for two hours, the store was ten minutes from closing, and still Jessica could not decide on the color she wanted the dress to be. The one Jari was holding up now was simple and beautiful, it's color pale.

Jessica glanced at Kara, her one and only bridesmaid. Kara grinned at her. "I'll try it on," she said, reaching for the dress and heading to the dressing room – a place she had been more than a few times. Jessica finally put the aqua-colored dress she had been considering down and followed Kara. Jari fell into step beside her.

"I like the peach because it is a muted color – it's not anything too vibrant. If you're going to have colorful flow-ers, it would probably be best to have soft colors for the wedding party. And, it's a solid, which is good. You don't want anything too busy," Jari advised. Jessica nodded thoughtfully, thankful for Jari's input.

Kara had flown in that afternoon for the sole purpose of finding a bridesmaid dress. Jessi was thankful Kara had come so that they could shop for a dress together, and had been delighted to have a reason for her to visit.

When Jessica had called and asked Kara to be her bridesmaid, the still pixie-ish blonde had been delighted. And not the least bit surprised, which Jessi liked. It con-firmed to her that their recently rekindled friendship was real and reciprocated. It was nice to know that as close as Jessi felt to her future sister-in-law, it was mutual.

During high school, Kara had become her best friend,

not only because she was Joe's sister, but because she was a beautiful person. Back then, Kara had been determined to be friends with Jessica, no matter how different they were or how difficult Jessica was to reach. Jessica had loved her for her persistence.

Since reconnecting last fall, their friendship had deepened as they found they had even more in common than they had in high school. They were now both women in helping professions with families of their own and a shared faith. Jessica smiled as she thought about how her friendship with Kara had grown and solidified. There was no one else she wanted standing beside her at her wedding.

"What's Jackson going to wear?" Jari asked. Jessica thought of the groomsman she had yet to meet. He was Joe's roommate from college and now played pro football, just as Joe would be if he wasn't so determined to fulfill his dream of being a pastor. Jessica thought again of how proud she was of Joe's diligence and determination.

"I think he'll wear a taupe suit with a white vest like Joe, and a tie the color of Kara's dress. The girls' dresses will be the same color as Kara's, too. Then we will only have white, taupe and one other color in addition to the flowers. What do you think?"

"Perfect. When you add in the color of the water and the sky, it will be gorgeous. Now, all we have to do is pick the color."

"Okay, ladies, here I come!" Kara warned, opening the door to the dressing room. The dress fell just past Kara's knees with a pleated, sweetheart bust, and an empire waist. The dress' sheer outer layer hung about an inch longer than the solid layer beneath, giving it a breezy, island feel. The pale peach was soft and tropical.

"What do you think?" Jari asked Kara.

"What does Jessi think? That's the real question," Kara answered with a laugh. Both blondes looked at Jessi.

"With a strand of pearls, it will be perfect," Jessi announced, releasing a deep sigh of relief as she beamed. It felt good to finally choose a bridesmaid dress. Poor Kara had already tried on so many. Jessica had felt wishy-washy and indecisive with each one. But not anymore.

Jari did a little dance that was very similar to the one Kelsi always did to celebrate, and Kara clapped her hands, bouncing up and down. "Really? You like it?"

"Yes," Jessi answered laughing. "Do you?"

"Yes! It's very comfortable, and I think it's perfect for a beach wedding. I wasn't so sure before I put it on, but now I think it's perfect."

As Jari went to Kara, gushing about how she agreed, how she had known it all along, Jessica's cell phone rang. She pulled it out and checked the caller ID, expecting to see Joe's number, or maybe Maybelle's as she was watching the girls. Instead, she saw it was her boss. There was only one thing that could mean. She flipped it open. "What's happened?"

"Tornados. In Arkansas. One flattened an entire town. There are still twisters all over down there. Homes have been hit, people are missing. Entire towns are literally being destroyed, Jessica." Her boss was out of breath. Jessi was sure the woman was already making preparations to leave.

"It's the beginning of February, Melinda. There shouldn't be tornados in February." Jari and Kara quieted.

"Exactly. People are in shock, Jess. Loved ones are missing, dead, buried in the rubble. Authorities haven't even begun to get a count yet on the dead or missing. Meet me at the airport in an hour. Can you make it?" Jessi thought of how long it would take to get home and then to the airport. It would be tight.

"Yes." With that one word, everything about her life for the next few weeks changed. Wedding plans halted, and the hurting people in Arkansas became her priority.

"See you there."

When Jessica hung up and turned, Jari and Kara were

watching her. Kara seemed concerned, but Jari was familiar with Jessi's work emergencies. "Where are you going?" Jari asked.

"Arkansas. There are twisters on the ground, whole towns destroyed," Jessi explained as she collected her purse and other belongings from the dressing room floor.

Jari nodded. "I'll pick up the girls from Maybelle's and go to your house to gather their things."

Straightening, Jessica gave her step-mom an impulsive hug. "Thanks, Jari!"

Jari returned her hug tightly. "You're welcome. You know I always love to have them! Kara, you can stay with us tonight, and the girls and I will take you to the airport tomorrow."

Jessica turned to Kara. "I'm so sorry that you flew all the way here, and now I'm leaving."

Kara shook her dress. "I came so that we could find a bridesmaid dress, and look! We found one! Mission accomplished."

Jessi laughed and looked at the peach dress again. "Yes, we did. I love it. You look beautiful."

There were quick hugs goodbye, then Jessi hurried through the store, jogged to her SUV, and headed home. She would throw some things together and, if traffic wasn't bad, make it to the airport just in time. While she was waiting for her plane, she would call the girls to say goodbye and tell them what was happening. She hated not being able to tell them in person and give them hugs, but they would be okay. They were used to her leaving unexpectedly. It would hardly be a disruption of their lives. Being with Jari was like being with a second mother in a second home. The girls loved Jari fiercely, and Jari returned their love wholeheartedly. Jessica smiled at the thought, thankful that the girls had such a woman in their lives.

She was grateful she had Jari so close. There was no way Jessica could have the job she did without her. There was no one else she felt more comfortable leaving her daughters with. She knew that when they were with Jari, they were carefully watched, protected and loved. And Jari was always interacting with the girls, teaching them something new, playing with them, or doing some kind of craft. The girls loved it, and so did Jari.

Her step-mom wouldn't be moving to Michigan with them. The thought hit Jessica like a ton of bricks and for just a moment, she found it hard to breath. When she regained her composure, she chided herself for her foolishness. Of course Jari wouldn't be moving to Michigan with them.

Still, as she pulled into her parking place, the realization that she and the girls would be leaving Jari – actually leaving her – brought her close to tears. She would miss her best friend. They had done everything together for over half a decade. Who would she do things with in Michigan? Who would she shop with? Go out to lunch with? Have family game nights with? And yet, as hard as it would be for her, she knew it would be even worse for the girls. Kelsi and Kamryn adored her.

Next to Jessica, Jari had been the steadiest and most present person in the girls' lives. She was there when they were born and had barely missed a day since. In fact, in some ways, she had been around more than Jessica. When Jessica had gone to college, the girls were with Jari. When Jessica flew to some distant place for work, the girls stayed with Jari. When Jessica worked out of her office, the girls stayed with Jari.

And for Jari, Kelsi and Kamryn were like the children she'd never had. She had helped feed them in the middle of the night. She had cared about every smile, every new tooth, every milestone, every monumental event, and even the ordinary days throughout the years. Her refrigerator was covered with pictures they had drawn, her walls were hung with photographs of them, her pool was usually full of pink and purple water toys.

Jessi felt her heart sinking as she realized how hard this move would be, not only for her, not only for the girls, but for the woman who had given up so much to make sure they had everything they needed. It would be a toss-up as to who would have a harder time with the coming separation – her, Jari, or the girls. One thing was for sure though – it would come with a lot of heartache for them all.

But now was not a time for reflection or sorrow. There was no time to dwell on anything in her own personal life. People were dying in Arkansas, and their loved ones were being left behind traumatized, wounded, and dazed, to pick up the pieces of what used to be their homes, towns and lives. And she was trained and passionate about helping them do just that.

Jessica pulled her car keys and hurried to the door of her building, calling for a cab as she did. In her apartment, she grabbed the bag she always kept packed, added her toiletries, and made sure she still had her purse. She left her car keys hanging on the peg in the kitchen, wrote a quick note to Jari, Kamryn and Kelsi, locked the door behind her and went down to meet her taxi.

At the airport, she met her boss, Melinda, and co-worker, Beth, at the entrance to the line for security. "One minute early. You're cutting it close this time," Melinda commented, checking her watch. Jessica smiled and took the ticket Melinda held out to her. "Did I catch you in the middle of something? Usually you're at least five minutes early."

"Shopping for a bridesmaid dress."

"Did you find one?" Beth asked.

"Yes, we had just found the perfect dress when I got the call," Jessi answered.

"Ooo! How exciting. What color?" Beth questioned brightly, momentarily forgetting the grim reality awaiting them in Arkansas in lieu of wedding news.

"Peach. It's beautiful." Jessi paused. "Where's Sally?"

"Not here yet. Oh, yes she is. I see her. There," Melinda said pointing, her expression grim.

Jessica looked to where Melinda pointed. The frazzled looking blonde whose coat was unzipped, scarf nearly falling off, suitcase skidding on one wheel, running toward them and waving, was definitely Sally. The woman was always in a hurry, always in disarray, but was one of the most genuinely compassionate and caring individuals Jessica had ever met.

When it came to helping people cope with tragedies in their lives, it didn't matter that Sally's clothes were rumpled, her schedule a mess, or that she was consistently five minutes late, because she was an expert at loving people. All that mattered was that when Sally sat down with someone, they walked away feeling heard, valued, cared about and loved. They had practical knowledge of how to move forward with their lives, and oftentimes, had already taken the first step.

Jessica hoped that one day she could be as good at helping people as Sally was. Even considering all the people Jessica came in contact with in her profession, all the good trauma psychologists she had met, Sally was her professional role model – rumpled, late and all.

"I'm here! I'm here!" Sally exclaimed as she crossed the remaining distance between them, already reaching for her ticket. Together, they got into line to move through security. Thankfully, the line was moderately short. "What kind of numbers are coming in? What do we know so far?" Sally asked immediately.

"Put your scarf on right. It's going to fall on the dirty floor," Melinda answered, pulling Sally's scarf even. She was as confident in Sally's counseling abilities as anyone, but everyone knew that Sally's disorganized ways annoyed their boss to no end. Sally tugged on her scarf and righted her suitcase to pacify Melinda.

"Thank you. Alright," Melinda started. "There have

officially been six twisters on the ground in Arkansas. It's been confirmed that two towns have been hit, one that has an estimated fifty percent still standing, the other only ten. The last I heard, twelve have been confirmed dead and dozens are missing." Melinda's face softened with compassion. "These twisters hit so suddenly, no one was expecting them."

Jessica absorbed the information as they moved through the line. Twelve people were dead, dozens more missing. Hundreds of miles away, there were people who were hurting, scared, in shock. The weather had turned against them to bring about a disaster they were not expecting to even be a threat for another month or two. Two towns, countless property owners, completely caught off guard, now surrounded by destruction and death. Jessica's heart ached for the people she would be coming in contact with during the days and weeks ahead.

Now that the twisters had hit, the damage would be assessed. People would need to come to terms with what had happened, grieve, pick up the pieces and begin to rebuild. If only it would truly be as easy for those involved as it was for Jessica to outline the steps that would ensue in the coming days, weeks, months and even years.

She set her purse in one of the plastic trays and lifted her suitcase onto the conveyer belt. She took out her earrings and dropped them in the tray, then slipped off her shoes and added them, as well. When motioned to do so, she walked through the metal detector and waited for her belongings on the other side. Once they came through, she collected her things, put her shoes back on and joined Beth.

Melinda was being subjected to thorough screening, as she was every time she went through security, due to the metal piece that had been used to strengthen her tibia after it was shattered in a car accident. Sally was still emptying coins and other miscellaneous items out of her pockets. Finally satisfied, she walked through the metal detector, only to hear it beep and realize she needed to take off her belt, too. She removed her belt, then the necklace her husband gave her that she forgot she was wearing. Finally, she made it through. "It's a typical day at the airport," Beth observed, amused. Jessica smiled.

By the time Sally rejoined the group, still trying to get her shoes and belt on, Melinda was checking her watch. "We have ten minutes, ladies. Let's boogy." Jessica pulled Sally's suitcase while the blonde threaded her belt through the loops on her jeans as they half-ran, half-jogged through the connecting terminal. They walked right up to the boarding gate, and when the plane started taxiing down the runway just a few minutes later, they were all safely in their seats.

Jessica sent Joe a text telling him they were taking off, she would call when she could, and that she loved him, before turning her phone off. She was glad she had called him during the cab ride to let him know what was going on. Unlike the girls and Jari, he was not yet used to her last-minute trips.

Seven

"Oh!" Sally's moan seemed to echo in the compact car, and Jessi pressed her hand against her stomach, trying to ease the pain that filled her. Beth sniffed, and Melinda cleared her throat. None of them could take their eyes off the mangled chaos around them that used to be a town – a town that had been home to so many. In just a few moments they would compose themselves, walk into a relief shelter and begin doing their jobs. But for just another moment, while they finished the drive through town to the shelter, they would allow themselves to absorb the shock and to mourn.

As far as they could see, there was nothing but debris. Though she had never been to this town before, Jessi felt certain this street had been lined with homes. Now, a mailbox stood as the tallest item on the street, beside what looked to be the start of a driveway. One car was left untouched, parked along the curb. A small flowerbed full of daffodils was unharmed. And yet there were no homes – only piles of rubble. Ancient trees had been snapped like twigs, some lying beside their stumps, others now on top of houses, and still others nowhere in sight. Cars which had been parked along the curb or in driveways were upside down, smashed, sitting on top of the remains of houses, and then, once in awhile, one looked exactly as it had when the owner had parked it.

Driving was difficult as the streets were as cluttered with debris as the lawns, the houses, and the town in general. A bulldozer had plowed one path down the street free of larger debris, enough so that emergency vehicles could make their way down the main roads. In that semi-cleared swatch was where Melinda now drove.

Search and rescue efforts were going on all around them. Jessi could see the workers, some in traditional uniforms, some in street clothes, others in bath robes and pajamas, steadily digging through the rubble. They worked quietly, hoping against hope that they could detect some noise, some cry for help and another survivor would be pulled from the rubble.

Jessica closed her eyes and wished for a brief moment that the sun could go back down to hide the damage. Their plane had landed in Little Rock in the middle of the night. After gathering their luggage, they had made their way to the car rental desk, and picked up their compact car. They had stopped for a much-needed cup of coffee before finding their way to the devastated town they had been instructed to report at. Nearly the entirety of their journey by car was made on windy, curvy roads that went up and down with the terrain of the hills, with corners sharp enough to keep Melinda's eyes wide open, despite her lack of sleep. The sun had just been coming up as they began their final decent into a large valley nestled in between the Arkansas hills.

As the sun touched the vast destruction, making clear the wide and horrible path of the tornado, Jessica's first reaction was to lose the contents of her stomach. Instead, she kept her eyes glued to the town they had dipped down into and focused on taking deep breaths. Supposedly, there were three more towns that looked every bit as bad, farther east in the valley. An expanse of land that had been a safe refuge, a place to stake out a home, the most logical place to settle, farm and build a community, had turned against the residents. The valley had given the tornado an easy path to follow, allowing its destruction to rampage the valley's residents.

"In all my years of working disasters, I've never seen anything like this. Look at how it just skipped around. The injustice would be maddening," Melinda observed as she turned right onto a road that appeared to have received very little damage.

Out of an entire town, only one street looked normal. Jessica let that fact settle. Here, houses rose up above yards that were just starting to green up, a telltale sign of the coming spring. A few patches of early daffodils were beginning to bloom, yet the tall oak trees were still waiting to spread their new leaves, a sign that winter weather was still a very real possibility. Cars were parked along the curb and in driveways. A few toys were scattered in one yard, and a pink tricycle sat just off the front porch of another house, waiting for its rider to come back.

Jessica could only imagine the residents' relief that their street, houses, lives and neighbors had been spared; all while dealing with the guilt that same reality brought. Why had they been spared when so many others had not? School crossing signs confirmed their proximity to the elementary school where a temporary shelter had been set up.

"It's a good thing the twister missed this. Otherwise, there wouldn't be anywhere left for a shelter," Beth said quietly as Melinda turned into the school parking lot. Jessica took a deep, calming breath as Melinda parked the car. She closed her eyes for a brief moment to pray. "Beauty from ashes," she whispered, reminding herself of the promise of God that she had clung to countless times.

Stepping out of the car, they headed toward the building. Only a few people were milling around the outside of the temporary shelter. The number would increase in the next several days and last for weeks. Right now, Jessi guessed, everyone who was able to walk was out searching for their neighbors, friends and family members; just as the four of them would be doing very soon. Jessica knew from experience that only those who needed medical attention or were unable to join the search and rescue efforts, whether physically or mentally, would be at the shelter now.

After going inside and assessing the number of people

seeking refuge in the school, Jessica turned to her boss. "If someone wants to man the shelter, I'll go out and work the fields." She knew the first twenty-four hours were crucial. Joining the search and rescue efforts was where she was most needed, and out there, in the midst of the disaster, is where she would come in contact with those who were hurting, shocked, and in need of someone who could help them cope.

"I'm going out, too," Sally stated, standing beside Jessica.

Beth nodded. "I'll stay here. I've already spotted a couple I'd like to make contact with."

Melinda nodded. "Good. Thanks for volunteering, Beth. Are you ready, ladies?" Jessi and Sally nodded. Jessi zipped her coat and pushed her hands into work gloves, glad she had put on an extra pair of socks in the car before slipping on her steel-toed boots. The last thing she needed at a disaster scene was to be unprepared and become another patient the medics had to take care of. She had learned early to protect her feet, her body, and her hands, especially when joining search and rescue efforts.

"Where do you need help?" Melinda asked, seeing a man in official search and rescue gear. The man glanced at their jackets, which identified them.

"Come with me," he told them tersely, his steps quick as he headed toward his marked vehicle.

~~~~~

"They were good people, they were. Always scooped my mama's sidewalk in the winter before they scooped their own. Sent their little ones over to do it, I think." Jessica glanced over at the middle-aged woman digging beside her. Rosetta paused in her searching, and Jessica saw the tears in her eyes. She knew the woman was wondering if she would ever see her mother's neighbors alive again, wondering if the little ones had survived. No one had seen or heard from any member of the family since a couple of hours before the twister hit. Their house had been demolished, but neighbors and friends were hoping they had gone out of town, hoping an emergency had drawn them to Little Rock or somewhere – anywhere – else.

"That was kind of them," Jessica answered gently. "How is your mother?"

"Oh, she's fine. She was over visiting her sister in Rogers, thank God."

"Yes, thank God," Jessi echoed softly.

"She was just about frantic trying to get in touch with me once she heard the news. She—" Rosetta stopped abruptly and swiped at her eyes, leaving more dirty streaks on her face. She took a deep, shuddering breath. "She didn't know if we had made it out alive or not. She just about fainted when I told her we were fine but that the house, the barn, the garage, was all gone. Ain't got the courage yet to tell her that her house is gone, too. I told her to stay at my Aunt Betty's for a bit longer. She's got a weak heart, and I'm afraid coming back here, seeing this..." Rosetta let her sentence dangle, but sniffed again.

Across the street, a shout went up. Jessica and Rosetta both turned to watch several people scramble across the rubble to help the man who was now digging in earnest, sending things flying over his shoulder.

"Oh, they must have found the Schobels!" Rosetta exclaimed, the joy in her voice evident. Jessica rejoiced in the fact that at least one member of the family must have been alive to cause the ruckus. She didn't let her mind dwell on the fact that one sound didn't ensure the survival of the entire family, or let herself wonder how many of the family members would be found alive, or what tragic story the survivors would be left with to carry with them for the rest of their lives. All that was important was that someone had heard a sound and that meant that somewhere, below the surface, in the midst of the rubble, someone was alive.

~~~~~

"He was just a baby." The stunned comment from the young woman in front of her made Jessi's heart ache, but she offered just a nod. The grieving mother needed to talk, and what she needed most was someone to listen. "It's funny how," Miranda paused and then continued, her voice wobbling, "two days ago, I was so tired and frustrated and I so wished that I lived closer to my sister so she could take him for just an hour so I could take a nap and now...." The young woman let her sentence hang unfinished as she sank to her knees on the debris that used to be her house and fingered the blue mobile that rose up from the chaotic mess of drywall, boards, shingles and insulation. Jessi watched Miranda swallow hard, holding back words that she could not yet bring herself to utter.

Aiden Hall, at eight-months-old, had been the tornado's youngest victim. When his single mom came to the shelter the afternoon after the deadly twister claimed the life of her only son, Jessica reached out to her. She recognized the loneliness Miranda felt – the young woman was lonely just as she had been before Joe came back into her life – and the guilt that overwhelmed her heart. The young lady was still numb, in shock, not really believing that her baby boy was gone, yet guilt had already taken hold. Jessica thought back just a couple of months to when she had stood in a hospital room, waiting to see if her own daughter would live or die. She had been overwhelmed with guilt, knowing her child might die because of her. Never mind that it hadn't really been her fault. The guilt was there, just the same.

Miranda had yet to open up or put voice to the emotions that were written so plainly on her face, but Jessi knew that at some point, she would. Jessica closed her eyes and briefly thought of the coming questions. Why had she decided to take a job working nights? Why had she left her baby with a teenage girl? Why had the twister hit while she was gone? Why hadn't she been there to take him somewhere safe? Why hadn't she been there to hold him tighter, to keep him from the mighty grip of the twister? Why was he taken when he was so young – when he still had his whole life in front of him? Why, if he was just going to die, had he ever been born? Why had God allowed something so tragic to happen? Why, when he was all she had, had he been taken away? Why, why, why?

Jessica bit her lip and remained quiet, mulling over the questions Miranda would ask, feeling the weight of each one. She prayed for wisdom to help answer such unanswerable questions, to help Miranda cope with reality, and to equip her with what she needed to one day begin to recover.

Jessi watched the first tear drip from Miranda's chin and get absorbed by the fabric of the mobile. That first tear broke the damn, and within seconds, Miranda was hunched over the item that used to hang above her baby as he slept, sobbing. Jessica rose and went to her, kneeling carefully on the debris beside her, putting her arm around the young woman's back. Jessi simply sat with her in her grief. Like in so many tragedies, there was nothing she could say to make it better, nothing she could do to make it right. But she could be there to let her know that she wasn't alone.

~~~~~

Jessica sat down on the side of her hotel bed, her cell phone in hand, with every intention of calling Joe and the girls. But when she took a deep breath, the tears came, and she sat with her head in her hands, crying. Throughout the day she was strong for everyone else, allowing herself to join those around her in their suffering. She was always the one pointing toward hope, a future, healing; but at night, all the grief, all the emotion, all the sorrow, needed to be released. Her head hung, her shoulders slumped, and she felt the weight of every death, every destroyed home, every piece of town history that had been ruined, every life that had been affected.

The whole town was grieving, not only for the twenty-three town members that had been lost – a devastatingly large number for a town where everyone knew everyone – but for the houses that had been destroyed, the softball fields that were now covered in rubble, the high school that was missing its left wing, the cars that had disappeared. Townspeople were grieving for the family heirlooms that were nothing but shattered pieces, the baby pictures that had been scattered across the state, the special baseball glove that was missing, the historic downtown that was nothing but a memory, the ice cream shop that the owners didn't have money to rebuild…. The list went on and on.

Sally was stretched out on the bed beside Jessi watching the news, but made no effort to join her or offer comfort other than to send her a sympathetic glance. Nights like these just came with the job and sometimes, when those helping had absorbed all they could, they simply had to let some of it go. Oftentimes, that took the form of tears that were shed for people they had never met, towns they had never been to and memories they had never experienced.

When Jessica's tears were spent, she felt ready to collapse from exhaustion. Instead of the phone calls she had hoped for, she settled for texting Jari and Joe, letting them know that she was fine and promising to call the next day. She knew Jari would understand. It was always like this the first week out. She hoped that Joe would understand, too. After changing into pajamas, she crawled between the sheets, set her alarm, and was asleep before she could reply to Joe's answering text.

~~~~~~

"I thought you might like something hot to drink." Jessica offered the steaming cup of hot chocolate to the young woman she had been watching for quite some time. Miranda had kept to herself for the past couple of days, and today she was sitting outside in the cold rather than spending time in the shelter or with the people still digging through the rubble. She sat against the outside wall of the elementary school staring out at a playground her son would never play on. She took the cup without ever glancing up and absent-mindedly set it on the ground beside her.

"I didn't want him, you know." Jessica didn't react to Miranda's blunt statement other than to slide down the wall into a sitting position next to her. Jessi hugged her knees to her chest, warding off the chill, setting her own cup of hot chocolate on top of them. "When I found out I was pregnant, I cried," Miranda continued, her voice dull and lifeless. Jessica waited for her to go on, but when she didn't, she took the lead.

"Why's that?"

Miranda sat and thought for several moments, then gave a slight shake of her head. "A baby just wasn't what I needed. Josh and I had just made the decision to get a divorce, and a baby only complicated what should have been an easy split."

"Is a divorce ever easy?" Jessi questioned thoughtfully.

"This one would have been, other than…"

"Other than a baby who gave you something to fight about? Something that couldn't be split fairly?" Jessi finished out of compassion. Miranda nodded, biting her lip.

When she didn't go on, Jessi probed. "What happened? Between you two, I mean? Why did you decide to divorce? Was married life so bad?" Jessi knew the baby's father, Josh, would be getting into town the next morning. He had been reached overseas and given leave from the military to attend his son's funeral. She also knew how much Miranda was dreading his arrival. Whether the dread came from having to be around her ex-husband or simply facing him after their child had died on her watch, Jessica wasn't sure. She aimed to find out, though, so she could help Miranda through the coming encounter.

"No, it wasn't bad at all. That's what made the divorce so easy." Jessica shook her head, not understanding, and a sigh that seemed to come from the tips of her toes slipped out of Miranda's parted lips. "We fell in love our senior year of high school. Everything was so easy, so right. He was comfortable. He made me laugh. After college, it felt like the natural thing to do was to get married. I'd been with Josh so long, I couldn't imagine not being with him. He was my best friend. I loved him." Jessica nodded, not completely able to keep a picture of Joe from her mind.

"We got married, and the first year was great. But then he had his first deployment, and honestly, it just stunk. At first, I missed him so much that nothing seemed to matter anymore. I didn't enjoy doing anything with anybody or doing anything at all. Nothing was worthwhile if I wasn't doing it with Josh. Then, slowly, as the weeks wore on, I realized that life went on, whether Josh was with me or not. I made friends. I got a new hobby. Over time, I learned to live without him." The young woman paused for several moments, then took a small drink of hot chocolate before continuing.

"When he got back, he was different. I felt like I didn't even know the man I was married to anymore. And I was different, too. I had learned I could do things on my own. I guess I didn't feel like I needed him anymore. I had learned to live without him, and frankly, I realized I liked it better that way. Everything he did started to annoy me, and I realized I didn't love him anymore. I had been head over heels in love with him in high school, even in college, but he was different and I was different and…it just wasn't there anymore. You know, Jessi, people fall into love and they can fall out. That's just how it was with Josh and me."

Another long sigh, another sip of hot chocolate. "At first he was hurt when I told him I wanted a divorce, but then he just accepted it. He knew, too. He knew we weren't happy together anymore. We were just better off apart, so we agreed to split up our assets, to be fair and civil about the whole thing, and go our separate ways."

"And then Aiden happened," Jessica stated, choosing to point out the obvious rather than a hundred other things that were hammering around in her head, thoughts of love being a decision, not a feeling. Marital advice was not what Miranda needed at the moment.

"Yes. Then…" Miranda paused. Jessi wondered if she would finally speak her son's name. "Then I found out I was pregnant."

"Did custody turn into a battle?"

"It was going to. It had started and then, well, Josh shipped out again before…he…was born."

Understanding came like the dawn. "Josh never met Aiden."

Miranda lifted one shoulder in an answer. "He was due to come back next month. I was dreading his homecoming, knowing we would have to talk about custody and visits again. I guess now we won't have to."

"Have you spoken to Josh since the storm?" Jessi asked gently. Miranda shook her head. "Are you scared to see him tomorrow?" Tears brimmed, accompanied with a quick nod.

"I just feel so guilty! Like I should have stopped it all from happening! I know that's how he'll see it. I know he'll blame me. And he's right. It's my fault. He never even met his son, and now he never will. I was the one who was supposed to be taking care of him, and I couldn't. I didn't."

Miranda only sucked in a quick breath before plowing on. "How do I even face him tomorrow? What do I say? Do I show him a picture and say, 'Hey, by the way, this was your son? He had your dimples and hairline. Maybe someday you'll have another kid that you'll actually get to meet.' How do I tell him that, Jessica? I wish the tornado could come back and suck me up, too. I wish I didn't have to face him. I wish I could have been the one to die instead of….Aiden." Finally speaking her son's name released a torrent of tears and Miranda bent over herself and cried, the grief rising up to consume her.

Knowing there would be time for words once the sobs slowed, Jessi again just put her arm around her new friend's back and let her cry – cry for the child she had lost, cry for the young life cut short, cry for her husband who would never meet his son.

In that moment, Jessi thought of Joe. How close had they come to being in the exact same situation? If things had ended differently, Joe would have never met Kamryn. Out of the blue, a troublesome fear worried at the edge of Jessi's consciousness. What if she and Joe, who had a similar story to Josh and Miranda, had the same ending? What if they woke up a few years down the road and realized that they were different people; that they were no longer best friends and that life was better apart than together?

Eight

"Hey Joe, it's Jessi. Sorry I missed you again. I know you're in class, but I got a free moment and thought I would at least call and leave a message. Things here are okay. I think in a way, we're almost past the worst of it. We're in our second day of funerals. They should be over tomorrow. After they're done…well, it's time to start moving on. I hope you're doing well and having a good day! I probably won't be around my phone much for the rest of the day, but I'll try to call again tonight," Jessi paused, and twirled a piece of hair around her finger. "I love you." She couldn't keep a smile from filling her face. "And I can't wait for May."

She hung up and slipped her phone back into her pocket, the now-familiar doubts coming with a rush and making her smile fade. She pushed away the sound of Miranda's voice saying that she and Josh had fallen out of love. Surely that wouldn't happen with her and Joe. Surely their love would last. Surely it was a decision and not a feeling. Surely their marriage would end differently. Surely.

Pushing away the thoughts about her own love life, she turned to go back into the shelter to find Miranda. Josh would be arriving in about ten minutes to meet with Miranda before the funeral for their son, and Jessi had promised the young woman she would be with her when he came.

Once inside, she waved to several people and promised to find them later. Grabbing a water bottle, she crossed the gymnasium to where Miranda stood against the wall. The woman was biting her lip, her arms folded tightly across her chest, her back pressed against the wall. Her eyes were closed, and Jessi wondered for a moment if she was sleeping while standing up.

"Is he here?" Miranda asked, taking a break from biting her lower lip.

"I haven't seen him yet."

Miranda gave a short, humorless laugh. "Do you even know who to look for?"

Jessica gave a slight smile. "I was thinking the crew cut and desert camies might give him away." Miranda grimaced. "Did you sleep last night?" Jessica asked, noting the dark shadows under the woman's brown eyes, but choosing not to mention them. Miranda shook her head no. "At all?" Another shake.

"I couldn't sleep. I kept wondering if this is all our fault. If God is getting even with us for the divorce...for fighting over Aiden. Like if we couldn't agree and be civil, He would just take him away. I wonder if it's my fault – if it's my punishment for not wanting him. If maybe he was a punishment all along – maybe he was born just so that I would love him and God could take him away to punish me." A look of sheer terror filled Miranda's face for just a moment before it was replaced by grim resolve. "He's here."

Jessica reached out and stopped Miranda before she could leave, unable to keep from addressing the woman's previous statements. "God delights in mercy, Miranda. This, Aiden, was no punishment. His life, no matter how short, was a gift, and God gave him to you as a gift. I don't know how this is good, because I know that it feels so very bad, but I know that God is good. His ways are good, and He is a merciful Father whose very essence is love, not revenge." Jessi knew her tone was almost beseeching, but the pain on the young woman's face was almost too much to bear.

Miranda's face smoothed out to pure disbelief. "Merciful? Good? If there is a God, those aren't the words I'd use to describe Him." With that, a young man in a suit was upon them.

"*Father,*" Jessi whispered quickly, sadly, before stepping forward to stand beside Miranda, letting His name express her unspoken prayer.

For a moment, Jessica didn't know what was going to happen. The man before them looked angry, ready to come unglued, and Miranda took a defensive stance. Before either of them could say anything, though, a small-framed woman at Josh's side, presumably his mother, cleared her throat. "Remember that you have *both* lost a son and the years of joy he could have brought you. Neither of you got to know him for nearly enough time. Parents were never meant to outlive their children." The woman's whispered words wobbled, and tears collected in every eye. Miranda's shoulders drooped, and the soldier's stance eased. Instead of making accusations, he reached out and pulled his young ex-wife into his arms. She instantly began to sob against his chest.

Jessica let out the deep breath she had been holding in anticipation of the coming storm, and swiped at her eyes. Josh's mother was standing back, letting the grieving parents have time to process together, and Jessica went to join her. With a kind smile, she took the woman's arm and led her toward the food counter. "Would you like a cup of coffee?" The woman nodded, wiping her own eyes with a tissue she produced from her purse.

"I haven't seen her since the divorce. I was so angry with that girl when she decided she didn't want to put the effort into their marriage. I was angry that she wouldn't try to find a way to love my son again. I was angry that she broke his heart. And I was so angry when my attempts to contact her to set up a time to meet my first grandchild went unanswered, but this…is no time for anger," the woman explained. "This is a time for grieving, and I will not let the two get confused. Confusing those two things will only make this more devastating than it already is." She wiped more tears.

Jessica handed her a cup of steaming liquid and then accepted one for herself from a Red Cross worker. Stirring her creamer in with a straw, she nodded. "You're very wise. I couldn't have said it any better. I admire how you turned that meeting in the direction that it most needed to go." Jessica reached out and squeezed the woman's hand. "I'm so sorry for your loss. So, so sorry." Aiden's grandmother sniffed. "I'm Jessica."

"I'm Alice. Are you one of Miranda's friends? Did you know Aiden?"

Jessi shook her head. "Alice, it's nice to meet you and sadly, no. I never met Aiden. I came to town after the twister touched down. I work with people who have gone through traumatic events. I help them cope with the pain and hopefully learn how to go on." Alice nodded slowly.

"Well, I think there's great need for you here, even in our small family. Josh and Miranda have been hurting and dealing with traumatic events since before the twister, before Aiden. Maybe somehow, this will eventually let them both begin to heal."

Jessi and Alice had just taken a seat at one of the tables when Josh stepped up beside his mother, Miranda not far behind. "Mom, it's time to go. The funeral will start soon." Alice stood, taking her son's arm for support. Jessica fell into step beside Miranda as they turned to make their way to the church. "Have you heard from your sister?" Jessi asked.

Miranda nodded. "She just called. Her flight was delayed, but she should make it here in time. This is one day I wish she lived just down the street rather than halfway around the world. It would have been nice to have her here over the past few days," she said as she dabbed at her wet eyes with a tissue. Knowing how true that was, Jessi slipped her arm around Miranda's waist and walked with her to her car.

~~~~~

The funeral was short, sad and beautiful. Jessi sat through it in a row with Melinda, Sally and Beth. Tears were flowing around the sanctuary as the town grieved for the baby boy who had been lost.

The pastor, even as he spoke words of hope and reassurance, seemed exhausted and ready to dissolve into tears at any moment. Jessi knew from experience that his faith was not necessarily wavering, rather the amount of sadness was nearly too much for this small town to handle. As the pastor of the people, he was feeling it acutely. This was his sixth funeral since the twister hit, and he still had many more to conduct.

Sometimes, in the midst of so much grief, hope was hard to cling to, no matter how strong one's faith. Jessi sat and prayed for the pastor, prayed for the family, prayed for the community.

~~~~~

"I think some part of him wanted to get back together," Miranda observed quietly. Josh and Alice had been gone for a little over ten minutes, having already left to drive back to Little Rock in order to catch their flight home in the morning. Miranda's sister was sleeping at her hotel, nearly passed out from jet lag. Now, Jessi and Miranda were sitting at one of the tables in the shelter, having coffee and debriefing from the day. It was late, and many of the lights had been turned off to allow people to sleep, if able. Many were plagued with nightmares, being forced to relive the terrifying event over and over in their dreams.

"Do you?"

Miranda shook her head. "I don't know. I know it felt good to have him here. I know I didn't feel so alone. I know it still felt like my best friend was back. But we don't always think rationally when we're grieving, so I told him I needed time – time to grieve before trying to sort out any feelings between us."

Jessica nodded slowly. "That makes sense."

"If we...if we did get back together...what if we had another baby? Another boy?" Miranda bit her lip, sounding afraid.

"You'll never be able to replace Aiden," Jessi said carefully, choosing her words with great thought.

"We could try. And we could tell ourselves that it's okay, that we never lost a son. Josh never met him and after time, he'll only be a memory for me." Miranda chewed on her lip for awhile. "I don't want to be with Josh again so we can get pregnant and have another baby in order to delete the last year out of our memories and pretend like nothing ever happened. I won't get back into a loveless marriage just so it can serve as a Band-Aid for our hearts."

"Sometimes, love grows where you plant it, water it and care for it," Jessi told her gently.

"But you have to have a seed. You have to have something to start with," Miranda objected.

Jessi bit her lip to keep from responding, knowing it wasn't the time or place. She swallowed the words that wanted to remind Miranda that she had been in love with her ex-husband, they had been married, shared their life together, had a child together – surely those were all seeds that, if nurtured, could turn into love again.

Obviously, Miranda didn't agree. She saw no future for them together. Her statement that she had learned to live without Josh and had begun to like it better that way, rang in Jessi's ears. Suddenly, personal doubts bombarded her. She had learned to live without Joe – she had done so for five and a half years. Was she foolish to think the love they shared as kids in high school would actually be enough to carry them through the years to come – years that would undoubtedly have rocky times, sad times and hard times? Would the love they found so long ago really last? Would it really be enough to carry their marriage through until death did they part?

Her mind raced ahead to difficulties that were sure to arise. Surely discipline issues would come up. There would be issues about how to parent the girls, how much to spoil them and how much to expect out of them. Would his guilt over being an absent father during their early childhood cause him to coddle them? Then there was the topic of moving. She had said she would, but when it came right down to it, Jessica didn't want to leave D.C., especially when there was so much uncertainty in their future. Finances would likely also add stress at some point. With that thought, for the first time, Jessi began to think in earnest about what life would be like in Michigan for her and the girls.

Joe worked, but was going to school full-time. He wouldn't be able to bring home a full-time paycheck, and with living expenses and having two children to feed and clothe, a part-time salary wouldn't be enough. She would have to work. She would have to start making inquiries, start applying for jobs, line up some kind of reliable child-care...the list seemed too long to handle at the moment.

Jessica forced her mind back to the conversation at hand and found Miranda watching her. "Where'd you go?" Miranda asked, curiously.

Jessi shook her head, clearing the last thoughts of home out of her mind. "I'm sorry, I just...I just followed a bunny trail. Was it good to have your sister here?"

Nine

Jari looked at Bill and nodded. She led the way out of the kitchen carrying one of the giant pink cupcakes with five candles, Bill right behind her with the other. Her cheeks hurt from smiling when she saw Kelsi and Kamryn's wide eyes and delighted, awestruck expressions.

She led the crowd in singing 'Happy Birthday' as she set her cupcake down in front of Kamryn, while Bill set his down in front of Kelsi. The girls' eyes were sparkling, their smiles bright, their faces alight with excitement.

"Make a wish, girls!" Joe said from across the table where he had his camera ready. All smiles, the girls blew out their candles. Jari clapped and cheered before going back in the kitchen to bring out the cake everyone else would be served. Several friends from school and their parents were there, as well as Tim, Carla and Maybelle.

Re-entering the large, formal dining room, Jari smiled as she located the girls, now both in Joe's lap, eating their cupcakes. Her heart swelled, and she was again thankful that even with their mother away, the girls had a parent at their birthday party.

Jari cut and served the cake, putting each slice on a pink plate. Carla added a fork and a scoop of ice cream, then passed the cake out to the guests. When everyone had been served, Jari sat down beside Bill and ate her own piece of chocolate cake. As she ate, she watched the sweet girls across the table and felt a familiar surge of love. They were so precious, so sweet, so innocent. Kelsi looked up, caught her eye and smiled at her, pink frosting framing her sweet smile. Jari smiled back.

Like a physical blow, it occurred to her that this might

be their last birthday party held in her dining room. This, in all likelihood, would be their last birthday in D.C. The fact that she felt ridiculous didn't keep the tears from springing to her eyes, and she blinked violently, hoping to keep them at bay. This was a happy event, not a time for tears. For a little while longer, she would still have her sweet girls with her. She had to focus on that.

Later that night, after the presents were unwrapped, the games had been played, the guests had left and the party remnants cleaned up, Jari took a cup of hot tea and went in search of the girls. She found them in the living room, nestled into an oversized chair with their dad. Joe was reading them one of the new books they had unwrapped earlier. Jari sat down on the loveseat beside Bill, crossed her legs and sipped her hot tea. Bill was reading the newspaper, and Jari laid her head against his shoulder, closing her eyes to listen to the story. Joe's voice was animated and Jari found herself giggling along with the girls. Even Bill chuckled once or twice.

When the story concluded, Kelsi hopped off the chair and ran to the entertainment system, bringing the remote control back to Jari. "What's this for?" Jari asked, her eyes sparkling. Kelsi's smile stretched across her face, and she glanced to her sister for approval. Kamryn nodded and giggled.

"My birthday wish is to have a dance party!" Kelsi told Jari, still grinning. Beside her, Bill chuckled, and Jari looked over just in time to catch the amused look he sent her way. Across the room, Joe looked curious.

"I don't know if tonight is the appropriate time for a dance party," Jari answered, feeling her cheeks grow warm.

"Why?" Kelsi demanded, sticking out her bottom lip.

"Kels, there are certain times that are great for dance parties and others that aren't," Jari said slowly, knowing the real reason for her hesitancy was her own vanity. She wasn't eager to look ridiculous in front of her future step-son-in

-law.

"Oh, come on, Honey, it's their birthday," Bill said, still chuckling as he gently urged her to her feet with a hand on her back.

"And it's my birthday wish," Kelsi added sweetly. Jari was reminded again that it would likely be the girls' last birthday in her home. Joe or no Joe, she surged to her feet and turned on the entertainment system, selecting the appropriate CD.

Kamryn jumped down, completely mobile again now that her casts were off, and joined them on the rug. Jari pushed the coffee table out of the way, and noted that Joe had settled back in his chair, with a grin, to watch.

As the music started, both girls started jumping around, dancing, laughing and squealing. Jari joined them, easily falling into their dance party routine. They jumped, twirled, pumped their arms and did the twist. She twirled first Kamryn, then Kelsi on her finger. They waltzed, they tangoed, they did the swing. Joe grinned, and Bill chuckled.

"Okay, everybody dance now!" Kelsi squealed. "Come on Grandpa! Come on Daddy! Everybody dance!" Convinced by expectant smiles and little girl tugs, both men eventually got up to reluctantly join the dancing.

Once on the dance rug with his daughters, Joe's reluctance quickly faded. Jari was proud as she watched Bill, too, make a conscious decision to forget about his image and join in on the fun with his granddaughters. There were years when he never would have considered dancing, no matter who had begged or how much. As Jari watched him twirl Kamryn around, doing some kind of odd jig she had never seen the likes of, she couldn't keep the grin off her face or gratitude from overflowing her heart. Her husband had turned into a good man.

Bill and Jari waltzed while Joe guided his daughters around the dance rug in a three-way waltz of their own. They square danced, two-stepped, danced hip-hop, and did the swing. Jari doubled over laughing as she watched Joe and Bill leap and twirl around the rug, doing ballet with the girls. By the time they all collapsed on the couches twenty minutes later, everyone was exhausted and laughing.

"Daddy, you should see it when Mommy dances with us," Kamryn told Joe, smiling.

"Oh yeah? Is she a good dancer?" Joe asked, his eyes twinkling.

Kelsi and Kamryn both nodded emphatically. "Last dance party she taught the girls how to disco," Jari explained, chuckling. Joe and Bill both laughed, imagining the scene.

Jari checked her watch and turned off the music. "Girls, it's almost nine o'clock – it's past your bedtime."

"But it's our birthday," Kamryn pointed out.

Jari smiled. "Yes, it is, but even birthdays have to end. It's time to call your mom and go to bed."

With only minimal protests, Kelsi and Kamryn crawled off the plush, oversized couch and headed upstairs. Jari stood to follow, but Joe stopped her. "I can put them to bed tonight, Jari. You've done so much for their birthday already. You stay down here with your husband and enjoy your tea," Joe finished with a wink.

Jari knew it was a nice gesture. He was only thinking of her, yet her heart sank. Of course their dad would want to put them to bed. Of course he would want that special time with them while tucking them into bed, praying with them and giving them goodnight kisses. And as their father, it was his right. She needed to let him do it. She forced a smile. "Okay. Thank you, Joe."

~~~~~

Joe chased the girls up the stairs and down the hall to their room, drawing a combination of shrieks and giggles. Once reaching their room, they leapt up onto the stepstool and jumped onto their big bed, rolling around and laughing hysterically, trying to escape his tickling hands. Finally, he flopped down on the bed beside them and pulled out his cell phone. He had promised Jessica he would call before putting the girls to bed.

He knew it had been hard for her to miss their birthday. It was the first birthday she had ever missed. Ironically, it fell on the first birthday he had ever been to. He knew she was thankful he could be there to make it special for them, but he had heard in her voice how much she wanted to be there, too. The girls were five and they had yet to have a birthday with both of their parents present. And as much as Jessi wanted to be there, he wanted her to be – as much for himself as his daughters.

It had been a month and a half since he had seen his fiancé, and he missed her greatly. He longed to see her, talk to her, hold her and kiss her. He wanted to ask what was bothering her, what that little something was that he could sometimes hear in her voice. Without having the luxury of spending the past six years with her, he wasn't sure if she was just tired, emotionally exhausted from work, or if something was wrong. Perhaps it was a combination of all three. He contemplated it again as he punched in her number. Whatever it was, he was going to uncover the source of it as soon as she came back from Arkansas.

When she answered the phone, there was no hint of a shadow in her voice, only excitement. "Mommy!" Kelsi and Kamryn cried jubilantly, together. She laughed, and Joe could picture her accompanying smile.

"Happy birthday, girls! How was your party? How were your cupcakes? Did you have fun?"

Joe grinned, listening to both twins recount the entire party to their mom, talking over each other and telling their stories in an impossibly high-pitched combination of words, laughs, giggles and shrieks. On the other end of the line, Jessica listened, catching as much as she could, asking questions about the parts she could make out. She laughed about their dance party, about Kelsi's description of Joe and

Grandpa Bill dancing, about Jari not wanting to dance when there were others present.

"Mommy, my wish before I blew out my candles was that you could be here for our birthday...or at least soon," Kamryn told her, and Joe heard Jessi's breath catch. Kamryn sounded so sad – such a stark difference from how she had sounded just moments earlier. Joe put his arm around the little blonde and pulled her close against his side.

"I know, Sweet Pea. I wish I was there, too. So much, Honey. I'll be home as soon as I can. It won't be much longer."

"How long?" Kelsi asked, her bottom lip quivering.

"Maybe a week," Jessi answered, her voice hopeful.

"That's still a very long time," Kamryn said sadly.

"I know. It feels like a very long time until I get to see you. I miss you...all three of you," Jessi said tenderly.

"We miss you too, Mommy," Kelsi and Kamryn said in unison.

"So does their dad," Joe added, with a grin.

"How were the cupcakes? Were they chocolate like you wanted?" Jessi asked, and Joe smiled as her bait worked. The girls took off again, talking about their cupcakes, their presents, and their birthday.

They talked for several more minutes and eventually hung up with I love yous and promises to talk again in the morning. Then the twins put on pjs, went to the bathroom, and climbed back up to lay beside Joe on the bed for a bedtime story, followed by a prayer. When Joe moved to sit up and leave the room, Kelsi grabbed his arm. "Will you stay and cuddle with us for awhile, Daddy?"

"Mommy always sleeps with us on our birthday," Kamryn added.

Joe considered the innocent faces and tried to determine if this were truly another tradition he didn't know about, or if it was simply a ploy to have him sleep in the big room with them. Deciding he didn't actually care which it was, he crawled under the covers between them, still in his jeans and button-up shirt. He had missed so many years, and yet now, a twin snuggled up on each side, it felt so right and natural to be their dad. Life was good. It would be even better once Jessica returned, the wedding was over and they all lived under the same roof.

~~~~~

Jari brushed her teeth, washed her face and changed into a silk nightdress. She put great focus into her bedtime routine, keeping herself from thinking about the one thing that tried to occupy her mind. She left a lamp on and crawled beneath the covers, folding them over her chest. She was glad Bill would be coming soon; tonight she didn't want to be alone. As if she had called him, he walked into the room. After getting ready for bed and turning off the lamp, he crawled under the covers beside her.

"It was a good party, Honey. You did a good job planning it."

She appreciated his approval, his words of affirmation. He hadn't always offered them so freely. "Thank you. I think the girls had fun."

Her husband chuckled in the dark beside her. "I know they did."

The quiet stretched and thoughts she had kept at bay came rushing back. The tears came, and she turned over, away from Bill, to shed her tears and brace against the pain in private.

"We can't make them stay, Jari." Bill's tone was gentle.

"I know," she answered, sniffing. "But that doesn't keep me from wishing they would." She paused for several seconds. "You expect to have to let children go at eighteen when they go off to college, not at five."

"They're not your children, Dear," Bill reminded, his voice still gentle even though his words were abrupt.

There was a long silence. Jari struggled to control her

tears and her voice. She knew that. She did. But sometimes knowing something and feeling it were very different things. She had been a part of the girls' lives from their very first breath.

Finally, she said the only thing she could. "They're the only children I have." As she dissolved into tears, Bill rolled over and held her, enfolding her in his arms and keeping her there until they both slept.

~~~~~~

"Is Joe going to be at the airport to meet you?" Sally asked, reaching over and patting Jessi's hand. Jessica had been fighting sleep for the last half an hour, trying to finish up paperwork that had to be submitted by morning. They were about two hours from landing at the airport in D.C. and they were both hoping to get in a nap before touching down.

"I hope not," Jessi answered absently. She didn't look up from her paperwork, and thus, didn't see Sally startle at the answer that was so unlike her.

"Why don't you want him to be there?"

The stewardess appeared at Jessi's elbow, asking for her drink order, giving her a blessed moment to think about how to formulate an answer out of the chaotic thoughts flying around in her head. She slowly sipped her ginger ale and waited for Sally to get her apple juice so the stewardess could move on. "I just need time to think, to let some thoughts settle."

"What thoughts? What do you need to think about?" Sally questioned.

Jessica took another drink. Her mind hummed over everything she had been thinking about, over everything Miranda had said. "What if getting married is a mistake?"

Sally looked taken aback, and shook her head. "There are a lot of 'what ifs' in life, and most of them stem from fear, not truth." Sally's simple answer made Jessi think. She stored her words away to think about later.

"My parents were in love when they got married. My grandma and mom both said so. My grandma said my mom was just like me."

"And?"

"And they're divorced."

"What are you saying, Jess?" Sally asked, her eyes narrowing slightly. "You love Joe Colby, don't you? Haven't you since you were in high school?"

"Yes, I do. That's exactly what I'm saying – maybe love isn't always enough." Sally opened her mouth to refute Jessi's statement, but Jessi interrupted her, suddenly feeling exhausted and overwhelmed at the thought of debating the subject. "I appreciate your concern, I really, really do. I just need to think things through. It's been an emotional few weeks for all of us. I'm tired, and it's probably just the exhaustion talking. I promise I won't make any life-changing decisions tonight." Jessi sent her co-worker a charming smile and elicited an amused one from Sally in return.

"You need to go home and sleep for a day, wake up, hug your girlies, and then sleep for another day," Sally conceded. "So do I. Although, I'll have my husband there to snuggle up to and debrief with. Nothing drains the negative emotions like a good talk with Curtis during a day out on the water on the new sailboat. Sure is a shame you don't have a husband to do the same with." Sally's wink drew a smile from Jessica.

"Okay, Miss. I get your point. I need to finish this paperwork, so I can start on that day of sleep you prescribed when I get home rather than staying up to finish this."

Sally fell quiet, allowing Jessi to resume her charting. She steadily plodded along through the pages of paperwork, reporting on her time in Arkansas. Before long, her pen stilled as her mind drifted back to the people she had left, people who were still grieving, who were still living in the chaos of a broken town and disrupted lives. They were just starting to look toward the future instead of being consumed with the past and the present. Although the journey ahead of them was long, when that switch happened, they were through their darkest days, and could begin to look forward. When insurance companies and FEMA stepped in to help rebuild, was when Jessi, Sally, Melinda, Beth and others like them, packed up and headed for home.

Jessi's thoughts turned to Miranda, and she found herself smiling at the memory of the young woman's hopeful expression as she boarded her plane earlier that day. With no husband, no child, no family, no house, no belongings – nothing but sad memories keeping her in Arkansas, Miranda quit her job, used her savings to buy a plane ticket, and took her sister up on her offer to live with her in Paris for awhile. When Miranda hugged her goodbye at the airport, she looked happier and more hopeful than Jessi had ever seen her. Jessica prayed it would be a good move for her. Honestly, she thought it would be, and she prayed that on her new journey, Miranda would come face to face with a God who redeems, who loves and who is always good.

Her thoughts turned personal, and she wondered if she would have had a hard time believing those truths about God if her own close call with Kamryn would have ended differently. How would she have responded if her child had died as Miranda's had? She hoped she wouldn't have lost her faith or accused God, but was not arrogant enough to discount the possibility. Though she was a believer, she was also still human and the enemy was crafty. She offered up a silent prayer. No matter what the future held, she asked the LORD to give her the grace to stay near to Him, remember truth, and remember His character.

Thankfully, it *had* ended differently. She thought of the two giggling, charming, pretty little girls she would pick up from Jari's in the morning. She smiled. If she wasn't so exhausted, she would ignore Sally's advice and go pick them up right away; however, she knew emotions were always harder to handle when exhausted, and seeing anyone when she was as tired as she was, wasn't a good idea. Which was why she had silenced Joe's calls for the past several days and responded to his messages with only basic texts, explaining she was busy with work. She was just tired. She needed sleep. Then, she would feel more like herself again.

The problem wasn't (and never had been) that she wasn't madly and deeply in love with Joe Colby. She had loved him since the day she met him and would never stop until the day she died. The feelings, the attraction, the need to be with him, were still there and just as strong as they had ever been. Her love for him was as strong as it was only a couple of months before, when she had accepted his ring, glowing and full of joy. But what if they were like the others?

What if love wasn't enough? What if the feelings faded? Or what if love wasn't enough to keep them from fighting? Or from going down different paths? What if they realized a few months into marriage that they didn't actually want to be together after so many years apart? The idea felt preposterous – she had never wanted anything more than to be with Joe Colby every waking moment of every single day. But still, if it had happened to so many others, could it happen to them?

Or, what if she remained just as in love with him, but he fell out of love with her? What if he wasn't satisfied? What if she wasn't the woman he thought she was? What if he started looking elsewhere? What if he would rather live life without her than with her? What if he started to resent the restraints put on him by being a husband and a father?

He had always lived a single life, always called his own shots, made his own schedule, done his own thing, and followed his own dreams without ever having to consult anyone else. What if marriage turned out to be more restrictive than he anticipated? What if he continued to do all those single things, even once they were married? Jessica wanted him to achieve everything he had ever wanted and would fight to make sure he got the chance to do so; but there were legitimate needs that would come with having a family – sacrifices he would have no choice but to make, sacrifices she had been making for years. Would he make them? If he did, would those sacrifices eventually cause him to resent her and the girls?

Her thoughts swirled, confusing and consuming her. The one question she kept coming back to was whether or not getting married was the right decision. Her mind stilled as she came to the echoing resolution that she would rather never have Joe Colby than to have him and lose him.

Ten

"Mommy, I'm glad you're home!" Kelsi sang out between bites of pizza. Jessica had gone to get the girls that morning, and they had been hanging out at home ever since leaving Jari's after brunch. The girls were content to play with their own toys in their own room, giving Jessi time to unpack and catch up on laundry. Then, they had all taken a nap together that afternoon. Jessi cherished the time spent snuggling with her girls. Sally was right. It was nice to have someone to snuggle up with after coming home from such an emotional job.

"So am I! I missed you girls so much!" Jessi agreed wholeheartedly. She treasured her small daughters and their time together. She was never more aware of that than after being gone. However, although she missed them, she didn't worry about them. They were in the best of care. Knowing they were with Jari while she was away, gave her peace. That would change if she moved to Michigan, she reminded herself sadly. How would she ever find anyone else who she could trust so completely with her girls? There absolutely could not be anyone else who could take care of them as well as Jari could.

"We missed you while you were gone," Kamryn added, after chewing and swallowing a pepperoni. "It seemed like an especially long time this time."

Jessi nodded. "It sure did."

"What happened, Mommy? Who were you helping?" Kelsi asked. "Jari said you would tell us about it when you got home. She said you were in Alaska."

"Arkansas," Jessi corrected, amused. She recounted the events of her trip, leaving out details that her five-year-olds didn't need to hear. She wanted to be honest with them and have them understand that suffering was going on in the world, but didn't want to overwhelm their tender hearts.

"We should pray for Miranda before bed tonight," Kamryn stated at the end of Jessica's story, and her twin agreed, still slurping down her root beer.

"I think that's a very good idea. Which movie should we watch tonight?" Jessi asked, helping herself to another slice of pizza.

"One with princesses in it?" Kamryn asked, her face lighting up.

"Okay, which one? One of the classics?" Jessi asked. Kelsi shook her head, holding her finger up while she swallowed her root beer.

"Jari got us that new one we wanted for our birthday. Have you seen it, Mommy? If not, could we watch it? You will like it."

"Oooo! Yeah, let's watch that! The horse is so funny," Kamryn agreed, squirming in her booster seat with excitement.

"All right, the verdict is in. We'll watch your new movie from Jari!" Jessica declared, drawing applause and cheering from her daughters.

"But not until after we call Daddy, right Mommy?" Kamryn asked, settling back in her seat to finish her dinner. She stabbed a leaf of lettuce and chomped on it, tilting her head, waiting for Jessi's answer.

"Absolutely. After we get the dinner dishes done, we'll call Dad, and then we'll watch our movie."

Jessi felt unsure about the phone call. Even after a good night's sleep and a nap, she didn't know how she was feeling about things. And a month ago, she had told Joe she would come for a visit once she was back from Arkansas. Would he remember? Would he ask her to come?

She was only partly paying attention to the happy chatter going on around her as she contemplated whether or not she wanted to see Joe. In a way, she wanted nothing more than to run into his arms, hug him tight, and let him hold her until he couldn't hold her any longer. She was just as pulled to him, just as drawn to him as she ever had been. Still, something inside of her held back. She wasn't sure what she was thinking, wasn't sure about their future, wasn't sure about almost anything, and she desperately needed clarity before seeing him face to face.

"Mommy, we're done! Who do you want to load the dishwasher tonight?" Kelsi asked, scooting out of her chair and heading for the kitchen, ready to move on with their evening. Jessica put her last bite of crust into her mouth and stood, brushing her hands off on her jeans. Kamryn hurried down from her chair to follow her sister, but paused to hug Jessi's legs.

"Thank you for the pizza and root beer, Mommy." Jessi stared down at the pale green eyes and beautiful smile on the small upturned face. She felt a smile start in her heart and work its way up to her lips. She loved being a mom. It was the greatest gift she had ever been given.

Would Joe feel the same way about being a dad? The thought caught her by surprise. "I would hope so," she murmured to herself as she bent down and kissed Kamryn's forehead.

"I'm just glad I was here to share it with you," she answered, then swung the blonde girl up to her hip and went to join Kelsi in the kitchen. The small brunette was already standing on a step stool, washing dishes at the sink. Jessi ruffled Kelsi's hair. "Look at you! What a helper you are, Kels! Thanks!" The little girl was all business as she kept scrubbing and ordered her sister to start putting the dishes into the dishwasher. Jessica laughed and kissed Kamryn's nose before setting her down to start her chores.

Ten minutes later, they were snuggled up on the couch with a blanket tucked in around them, the movie paused at the beginning. Jessi dialed Joe's number and listened to it ring twice before his familiar voice came across the miles separating them, filling her living room.

"Hey Joe," her voice was tender, more full of emotion than she had meant for it to be. She was glad when the girls erupted in joyous greetings, giving her time to get herself under control. They had only chatted for a few minutes before Joe brought up the very thing she had been dreading.

"So, Jess, when do you think you three beautiful ladies will be able to come to Michigan?" he asked.

"Tomorrow? Mommy, can we go see Daddy tomorrow?" the girls instantly asked, turning pleading eyes up to Jessica. Joe chuckled on the other end of the line. Jessica tried to hide her irritation. Had he asked when the girls were listening so she wouldn't have the option of saying no?

"Flights would be very expensive if we went tomorrow," Jessica answered slowly.

"Nope, I already checked. There's a last minute deal from D.C. to Grand Rapids. It's only a hundred and twenty dollars per person. It doesn't get cheaper than that. Flights into Grand Rapids are expensive." Again, Jessica had to temper her irritation as he promptly shot down her best excuse.

"That is pretty inexpensive," she paused. "The thing is, I just got home. I haven't caught up on sleep yet and—"

"Well, then this idea is perfect," Joe continued, undeterred. "Come get rested up here. The girls and I can hang out, and you can sleep. Even if you sleep for the entire time you're here, at least we'll all be together as a family."

"Yay!" There was more applause and cheering from the five-year-old section. Out of excuses, Jessica threw up her white flag.

"Alright. When does the flight leave?"

"Eleven o'clock tomorrow morning. You should get in at half past three, which is perfect, because I get out of class at a quarter to two. I'll pick you up!" Joe sounded as excited as the girls, and Jessi tried to convince herself that she should be excited, too. If the three people she loved most in the whole world were this excited, surely she should be also.

The conversation ended ten minutes later with promises to see each other the next day. Jessi turned on the movie before the girls could start discussing the phone call or the upcoming trip, and relished the chance to turn her mind off and watch the animated story. Even though she tried to stay awake, she fell asleep before the movie was over and woke up to find the credits rolling across the screen. She smiled tenderly as she realized both girls were also asleep. She stood, carefully lifting one at a time, and carried them to bed.

Once the girls were tucked in for the night, she thought about packing, but exhaustion won out. As she fell into bed, she determined she would get up early and pack.

Eleven

Jessica kissed the girls goodnight and then straightened, standing still for just a moment to let her knees adjust. After her fall on some rubble in Arkansas, her left knee still protested if she bent it for too long.

The girls were bedded down on the floor on either side of Joe's queen-sized bed. As Joe finished telling them goodnight and pushed himself to his feet, Jessica glanced around his tiny bedroom and sparse furnishing. She noticed that there was barely room for a five-year-old to lie on either side of his bed. Again, emotions churned inside of her, and her mind started to fill with confusing thoughts. She turned out of the room and headed to the kitchen where dinner dishes still sat on the counter. She ran a sink-full of soapy water and reached for the first pan.

"Hey, I'll get those," Joe told her, coming into the kitchen. "You sit down – you've had a long day."

She felt herself bristle. "I know how to wash dishes, Joe."

He hesitated before answering. "I know you do. I didn't mean to insinuate that you couldn't wash them. I simply want you to sit down and relax because I know how tired you are," he said slowly.

"Well, I'd rather just get them done real quick," Jessica answered, reaching for the next pot and dunking it into the sudsy water. "Then we can both sit down and spend time together." She added a quick smile at the end.

Jessica tried not to react as Joe came to stand beside her, his back against the counter so he could see her face. He stuffed his hands in his jean pockets and studied her face for several long moments before speaking. "What's going on, Jess?"

"What do you mean?"

Joe blew out a breath. "Well, ever since I picked you up from the airport this afternoon you've been distant, almost snappy."

She shrugged. "I'm sorry, I'm just tired. Going out of town for so long exhausts me. It's a part of my job, Joe, and it's probably going to happen again. Often, actually. If you can't handle that, well then…" Jessica let her sentence dangle as she moved the rinsed pot to the dry towel on the counter. She reached for the closest plate.

"Well then, what?" Joe prompted.

She sighed. "I haven't spent more than thirty-six hours at home in the last month."

He reached out and rubbed her arm. "I know. I can understand that you're tired. Maybe this weekend will get you rested up." He flashed her a grin. "Let me take care of you and the girls for a couple of days. You recuperate. That's part of being married – you're not alone anymore. You don't have to do everything by yourself anymore, Jess." He grabbed another clean towel and used it to hit her gently on the backside. "Including the dishes."

Jessica couldn't stop it before it came out. "We aren't married yet, Joe." She instantly wished she could take it back. It had sounded so matter-of-fact, so cold. She saw him flinch out of the corner of her eye.

"What do you mean?"

"What do you mean, what do I mean?" she asked, forcing her voice to stay calm and even. He didn't answer, only stared at her, his expression revealing his hurt. "Obviously, we aren't married yet, unless I missed the wedding and the honeymoon. It's not a confusing statement."

"Well," Joe hesitated. "What are you implying?"

Jessica scrubbed the plate furiously. "I don't know."

Joe put down the pot he was drying and turned her toward him by the shoulders. "You don't know? Jess. What's going on? You're worrying me." She met his pleading gaze.

"Joe, I'm going home the day after tomorrow. Home. And you're staying here. I can't let my guard down. I can't play house for two days and pretend like all I have to do is to be a mommy and a wife, then get to the airport and re-member, 'Oh no, I'm a single, working mother with two daughters, an office that I have to go into Monday morning and once again, I'm all alone.' We're here this weekend, yes. You were in D.C. over Christmas break, yes. But we aren't married yet. I'm a single mom. I have to do things myself, take care of myself...so don't tell me that I don't."

"Maybe until May, that's true. But this weekend you're here, with me. Let me take care of you. If you'll let me, I can step into that role right now...at least until you have to leave."

Jessica let him pull her into an embrace, and after a few moments, she could feel the tension that had filled her begin to ease. She let her head sink to his shoulder. "I'm sorry. Really, I'm so sorry. I'm just so tired I can't think straight." He kissed the side of her face so gently she felt herself melt a little more. Then he released her and took the dishcloth from her hand.

"Go to bed, Love. I'll finish up in here." She shook her head. "The girls are asleep, and I don't want to waste this opportunity to spend time with just you."

His smile was so tender it almost hurt her. "There will be time for us tomorrow. Right now, you should get some sleep. I'm serious."

She knew he was right, knew that if there was any chance their weekend was going to turn out well, she needed to erase some of the exhaustion that intensified eve-rything she was feeling. Conceding, she stretched up and kissed him. "You're right. Thank you. I'll see you in the morning."

Joe smiled. "Sleep well."

Lying in bed five minutes later, Jessica's mind raced.

She wanted to sleep, but all she could do was worry. She was worried about moving to Michigan, about the conversations she and Joe needed to have, about whether or not the girls would be quiet at the museum the next day. But most of all, she was worried about Joe.

When he told her earlier that she wasn't alone, she had wanted to scream at him not to ever tell her something like that again – not when she and the girls were leaving in forty-eight hours. She would be right back to cooking dinner alone, playing games with the girls alone, tucking them into bed alone, cleaning up the kitchen alone, going to bed alone, waking up alone. Whether he wanted to admit it or not, they weren't married yet. Engaged, yes. Married, no. Even with reservations for May in St. Lucia, nothing was concrete. Sometimes, things happened.

After five years of being a single parent, and her first sixteen years of being on her own for all reasonable purposes, she couldn't let her guard down, couldn't let herself get too dependent on anyone else, not even Joe. Not until it was for sure. "Don't count your chickens before they're hatched," was what Pops used to say, and even now, even with Joe, she couldn't do it.

She knew her response in the kitchen had hurt and greatly troubled him. His smile was so tender, but it was also laced with pain. He sent her to bed because she was exhausted, but she knew it was also because he didn't know how to go forward with the conversation. He needed to think. She needed to think. Her quick comment had made it all too clear where she was in her heart. It made it all too clear that there were no absolutes in her plans for the future. Everything was still up in the air, and he now knew it.

Still, she didn't know what to say, didn't know how to explain it to him in a way he could understand. She didn't know how to put words to what she was feeling. Even if she did, so often lately, she felt like he took anything she said as a direct criticism against his ability to be a good father or to lead their family. She understood that he hadn't had the time with the girls that she had. She understood that it was all new to him, and he was trying. She loved him for it. She thought he was doing a great job. But anytime she tried to explain any of her doubts or fears or even just discuss thoughts or valid concerns, he took it so personally.

And what she really wanted to explain was that more than anything, she loved him – down to the very core of her being. But she was scared. Plain and simple.

Additionally, she didn't feel like she knew this new man she was engaged to. She loved him, because she knew deep down who he was. She knew his character, his accomplishments, his heart. But she didn't know what his favorite restaurant was or if he had a favorite shirt. She didn't know what he usually did on the weekends or where he spent his last summer break. She didn't know how he voted, if he watched television every night, or what he did to stay fit. Did he go to a gym? Did he go on runs? She didn't know. She didn't know if he liked an aisle seat or a window seat on a flight, or if he ever had a glass of wine.

And she didn't feel known by him. She knew that he loved her, but he loved her based on the girl she was in high school. That girl had long since been replaced with a woman…and a mother. She had changed. She wasn't foolish enough to believe that his love didn't extend to her now, or that he wouldn't love her if he knew her. She knew he would, he always would, because their love had been real and, in fact, it was still real; but she wanted to know him and be known in return.

She didn't blame him. When they had spent so long missing each other, it was hard to admit that they needed to get reacquainted. With the girls always around, it was hard to have the conversations they needed to have. And in all honesty, she had been avoiding him for the last few weeks. With being parents to the same children, their wedding just a couple of months away, and the very real love they had for one another always at the forefront, it seemed like the most unnatural and impossible time to begin dating and getting to know each other again. But it's what she longed for. It's what she needed. And she needed it to happen before the wedding.

Knowing they were deeply attracted to one another and shared a mutual respect and love, she had often wondered if getting to know each other again might become one of the joys of marriage. Still, a niggling fear told her that it had to be done before they were married. What if they realized they were two very different people? What if they discovered differences too big to bridge? What if, once they got to know each other again, he decided he liked life better without her? That maybe marriage wasn't what he wanted? Her heart raced at the thought, and her throat burned.

Jessica stared up at the ceiling, trying to sort through her emotions. The one feeling that overtook all the others was a longing to be with the man she was about to marry – to be with him forever. He was intriguing and electric, and she felt as pulled to him as ever. She wanted to know him – know his quirks, his likes and dislikes, what made him tick, how he thought and what he felt. She wanted to know the new Joe Colby – the man, not just the boy.

Why, if the only thing she wanted was to be with him – to know and be known by him – why was she so close to calling the entire thing off?

~~~~~

Joe turned off the light, made sure the front door of his apartment was locked, and stretched out on his living room sofa. It wasn't nearly as comfortable as his bed, but it worked. He was more than happy to give up his bed for a couple of nights if it meant having Jessi and the girls around.

However, this weekend was already going very differently than he had imagined. Before leaving to pick them up from the airport, he had put a pan of lasagna in the oven. He had followed his mother's directions exactly, yet had not accounted for how long it took to get two five-year-olds through an airport, collect luggage, walk through the parking lot, drive home in rush hour traffic, stop for a potty break at a gas station and carry the luggage up to his apartment. The lasagna he had so carefully prepared in hopes of making his family the perfect dinner, had filled his house with smoke and burnt to a crisp. Thankfully, the fire alarm in his apartment didn't work and saved him the mess of the sprinkler system thoroughly dousing his belongings. Jessi had cooked a quick meal of spaghetti to go with the salad he had tossed, but he didn't have any milk for the girls. They had grudgingly settled for water with their pasta.

The trip to a nearby park and then putting the girls to bed had gone smoothly enough, but it had been followed by the awful conversation in the kitchen. He thought back to what he had said, what she had said, what he saw in her eyes and what she had wanted to hide. It didn't matter that she had relaxed in his embrace, that she had kissed him before bed, or even that she protested sleep on the grounds of wanting to spend the evening together. In the depths of her eyes he had seen doubt and it cut him to the core.

When she stated that they weren't married yet, there was no anger or bitterness in her face. And in the most obvious sense, she was completely right. In such a simple, correct statement, there should have been nothing to question, nothing to object to, nothing to worry about. But the way she had said it, as if everything was up for debate, combined with the doubt he saw in the depths of her blue eyes, was something that troubled him long into the night.

Twelve

"So, I bet you girls are glad Mommy's home, huh?" Joe asked as they walked through the park on their way to the jungle gym. He held a small hand in each of his, and Jessica was walking leisurely alongside Kammy. She tipped her face back to enjoy the sun as they walked, thankful that the uncommonly warm March day had come during their visit to Michigan.

Michigan. The place they would soon be living.

"Yes!" the girls answered in unison, shooting charming smiles at Jessi.

"I'm just as happy to be back," she told them. "I don't like to leave you girls for that long."

"We know. We don't like it either, but we have a good time with Jari and Grandpa Bill. We like it there. We have fun. We play games and eat ice cream, and Grandpa gives us candy when Jari isn't looking."

Joe laughed. "No wonder you like it there!" The girls giggled. "Well, you may not get to go to Jari's anymore when you move to Michigan, but it will be nice having Mommy home with you all the time, right? And I'll get to be with you every night."

The girls looked at Jessica as if their heads were on a string she pulled. "You're going to stay home all day, Mommy? Every day? You won't have to go into your office anymore when we move to Michigan?"

Jessica couldn't help shooting Joe an irritated look. He had gotten the girls' hopes up for something that was not even a possibility in the near future. Now, she had to be the bad guy and say no. "Well, girls, sadly I don't think that's actually going to happen. At least not right away."

"Why? Daddy just said it would," Kelsi asked, looking up at Jessica out of curious green eyes. They stopped and stood by a bench on the edge of the jungle gym.

"Yes, why?" Joe questioned as well.

Jessica blew out a frustrated breath, and shifted her attention back to the girls. "Well, we'll just see what happens. Why don't you girls go play? They have monkey bars over there. Do you want to show Daddy how you can cross the monkey bars?"

The conversation forgotten, Kelsi and Kamryn sprinted across the gravel to the monkey bars, instantly falling into easy chatter with the other kids who were playing. Jessi took a seat on the bench to watch them as she had so many times over the past few years, but this time Joe sat down beside her. He turned toward her, propping one arm up on the back of the bench.

"What do you mean you don't know if you'll stay home with the girls?" Jessica took a deep breath. This was the conversation she hadn't wanted to have, yet it needed to take place.

"Joe, I don't know how it's going to work."

He shook his head. "How what's going to work?"

"This! Michigan, me staying home...us...."

"Jess—"

"Hear me out," she pleaded, and Joe nodded in concession, yet she saw that she had already hurt him.

"When I was in Arkansas, I did a budget. With basic living expenses only, we're not going to have enough. Plus, we would have to get a new apartment. There's no way the four of us can squeeze into yours. Not long-term. Where would the girls sleep? Where would all of our furniture go?"

"I know. I figured we would need to," Joe agreed, running his hand through his hair.

"But we can't afford a different one, not with you going to school and me staying home with the girls. Where would our money come from? I know you have that part-time job, but it's not enough."

"I'll get another part-time job, or a full-time one."

Jessica shook her head. "When would you have time to study? When would you have time for your classes? When would you have time for us?"

Joe looked out at the playground for several long moments. She could tell he was trying to process what she was saying, trying to come up with some sort of a plan that made sense, and she stayed quiet, letting him think. He turned back to her.

"Okay, so maybe you go back to work until I'm finished with school," Joe said slowly, as if realizing his best made plans weren't realistic.

"That's the logical conclusion; however, Joe, I can only do the job I do because of Jari. I can only work at all because of Jari. Do you know how much good, quality daycare is? Then times that by two. Even with the girls starting school next year, we would still have to pay for after-school care. With that and work expenses, we still wouldn't have enough, even with me working. Not to mention, I don't want to put the girls in daycare. Leaving them with family is way different than putting them in daycare." Joe nodded his agreement. "Besides, I have to travel with my job. A lot. What will we do with the girls if I have to be gone for a month? They can't go to class with you or to work, which are both things you have to do in the evenings sometimes. And when would you get your studying done?"

Again, Joe sat quiet for several long moments. Jessi turned to the playground and watched her small daughters running around, laughing and playing. The March sun was unusually warm and warmed her on the outside, yet inside she felt cold. Her engagement, her long-awaited life with Joe Colby, was unraveling. This was supposed to be a magical time in their lives, a wonderful, hope-filled, beautiful time, but it was turning out to be too good to be true. She bit her lip against the pain of her sinking heart.

"I can't quit school, Jess. I've worked too hard for too long."

She turned, surprised by his quiet, pain-filled answer. "I never asked you to. I would never ask you to. I want you to have everything you ever dreamed of. I want you to do what the LORD has called you to do." The silence stretched again.

"I really have thought about this," Joe finally said. "This isn't new information to me. I just think that something will work out. I have to be with you, Jess – you and the girls. There has to be some way to make it work."

Jessi bit her lip. "I want to be with you, too, with everything that I am, but—"

"But? We're getting married in two months, Love. How is there a 'but'?" he interrupted.

Jessi didn't know whether to feel defensive or just weary. "I have kids, Joe. I have to be practical. You don't understand. If we don't have money, how will they eat? What happens when their jeans get holes in the knees? How do I take them away from their family – away from Jari who loves them and they love her, and leave them at some sterile daycare where they are one of thirty kids to teachers who are simply doing their job? I can't do it."

"Jess," the pain in Joe's voice made her cringe. She wasn't trying to hurt him; in fact, it was the last thing she wanted to do, but there were real issues of practicality that needed to be addressed. She couldn't move away from her family and her life because she loved someone, without any thought to how it might affect her children. First and foremost, she was a mom. Tears stung her blue eyes. Joe reached out and ran his thumb down her cheek, then lifted her chin to force her to meet his eyes. "Love, this is going to work out. It will be alright. I love you, and I know we're supposed to be married. We're supposed to be a family. The rest will fall into place, you'll see."

Jessica turned her face and looked down, tears welling

up in her eyes. He wasn't getting it. He wasn't understanding what she was saying. She couldn't do it. She couldn't move the girls without something stable waiting for them. At this point, they had a one bedroom apartment and a part-time job. That wasn't enough for a family of four. And Joe wasn't understanding. How could he? What she was trying to say was getting lost in translation. They weren't communicating as well as they had when they were in high school. It had been so easy then – it seemed as if they could read each other's thoughts. Now everything just felt murky and confused.

Jessica checked her watch and stood, taking a deep breath. "Girls!" she called. Kelsi and Kamryn stopped in their play and looked at her. "Come on, time to go," she told them, motioning for them to come. The girls sprinted toward them. Joe stood up and slipped his arms around Jessica's waist.

"Jessica, it's going to be alright. It really is. You have to trust me. Trust God to work it out. You're just scared, Love, that's all." She stepped out of his embrace and tried to plaster a smile on her face.

"We have to go if we're going to catch our flight."

~~~~~

Joe felt truly confused, unsure and afraid for the first time since the days when they weren't sure Kamryn would survive the accident. He reached for Jessica, but she stepped farther out of his reach and turned to the girls as they approached, asking if they'd had a good time. Joe tried to reach for her hand, but she expertly stepped around Kamryn, putting the little girl between them. Their daughter eagerly grabbed his hand and held it all the way to the car, chattering gaily, just like her sister on his other side.

Joe could barely manage to stay tuned in to the conversation going on around him. What was Jessica doing? Was she really going to leave like this? What did it mean if she did? Was this why she had been so distant for the last month, and especially over the weekend? Was this why he had felt

like she was a thousand miles away last night when they cuddled on the couch during a movie?

In high school, it had been so easy to figure her out.
Back then, it was like he held a map to her heart. He had always known what to do to get through to her. It had been like
that again at Christmas, but the last few days it felt as if she
was a locked box, and he no longer held the key. No matter
what he did or said, he could not reach his fiancé. Yet, today's conversation was the first thing that had caused great
fear in his heart.

"Daddy! Are you going to unlock the door, Silly?"
Kelsi asked, tugging on his hand. He realized they were
standing beside his car.

"Of course." He unlocked the doors and opened Jessica's first, then the back door for the girls.

Once inside, Jessica reached over and put her hand on
his arm. "I didn't mean to hurt you...I don't ever want to hurt
you. Please know that's never my intention." Joe looked at
her, his mind and heart reeling. Her eyes were sad, a sadness
so deep that his heart responded in fear.

"Please don't leave like this. Not with this conversation
unfinished." His voice was close to pleading. Why was he
having to beg his fiancé not to leave on bad terms? Shouldn't
she want to clear things up, too? Hadn't she wanted this
weekend to go differently? Surely she hadn't wanted things
to end up like this. They were getting married in two months,
and yet she didn't seem like a woman in love.

The girl who held his heart in her hand simply looked
away. "We have to catch our plane. We don't have any more
time. And you have youth group tonight."

Joe's heart started racing at the same time that it plum-
meted. He drove quietly though traffic, trying to think, trying
to process what was happening. This wasn't the end. This
was an off-day, an off-weekend. Every couple had them. He
forced himself to inhale slowly. This wasn't a huge issue, it
was simply a disagreement. In fact, it wasn't even a disagree-

ment. She was just scared. It had happened enough in high school, and they had survived. She just needed to be held, reassured. She needed to know that he loved her, and that he would take care of her. That was all. But every time he had tried over the past few days, she distanced herself from him as if she wasn't buying any of it. Or it was no longer enough.

Was he not enough anymore? Did she no longer think he could take care of her? Didn't she think he could provide for her? They were about to get married, yet she had plainly stated that she was going to have to be the provider. She had clearly insinuated that she was the only one who knew what the girls needed. She was the only one who could properly care for them. She was the only one who had their best interest at mind. He blew out a frustrated breath as he veered onto the airport exit, feeling deflated and defeated. She was leaving and that was that. They would have to work it out long-distance or wait for the next time they saw each other, which could be a few weeks or even a month away.

Joe checked the clock and decided to pull up alongside the curb in the unloading zone rather than parking, considering how soon her flight left. Going to the park really had pushed the limits of their timeframe. He had thought it would be a great chance for the girls to burn off some extra energy and for him and Jessica to clear the air before her flight home.

Home. He couldn't wait for the day when her home was with him, when they didn't have to leave each other anymore.

Jessica nearly jumped out of the car as soon as the vehicle came to a stop and opened the door for the girls, racing around to the back to get their luggage. He got out slowly, irked that she hadn't waited for him to get her door or the luggage and hurt that she was clearly in such a hurry to get away from him. Obviously, getting the car door and lifting the luggage out of the back weren't things she thought him capable of doing, either.

"Girls, give your dad a hug goodbye," Jessi said, her smile too bright to be sincere. He wondered if she thought he didn't see through her. Joe reigned in his thoughts to focus on the girls for their goodbye, which brought tears and sad faces. He was not ready to let them go, and he held them for several long moments. "Okay, girls, come on. We have to catch our plane. Let's hurry," Jessi encouraged, all business. Joe reluctantly released his small-framed daughters and straightened.

It surprised him when Jessica came to him, wrapping her arms around him and holding him close, resting her face against his neck for several seconds. "I love you," she told him, pulling back and looking up into his eyes. Her blue eyes were so sincere and clear, windows to her heart as they hadn't been all weekend. He could see her love for him shining in them, and for a moment, he thought everything was going to be okay after all.

But when she squeezed his hand, then released it, she left something in his palm and closed his fingers around it. He looked down and his heart sunk. It was her engagement ring.

"It's just not going to work. I'm sorry. The wedding is off." Joe looked up slowly, feeling stunned, as if he was moving in slow-motion while everything around him continued as normal. Jessica turned and walked away, herding the girls in front of her. But before she turned, he saw the tears that filled her blue eyes.

"Jess, don't," he groaned, his voice sounding as if it stemmed straight from his breaking heart. "Please don't do this." She kept walking, and belatedly he regained his senses and started after her. But she had already disappeared into the airport. Behind him, people were honking, and a security officer had started in his direction, letting him know he had been parked in the unloading zone for too long.

He looked down at the ring again, feeling close to tears, and nodded slowly, slipping it into his pocket. He got back into his car and pulled away from the airport.

Thirteen

"When will we see Daddy again?" Kelsi asked sleepily from the backseat of Jessi's SUV. Jessica swallowed hard, feeling weary and unable to make it through the next twenty minutes. She wanted to lock herself in her room and release the tears that had made her throat ache and her eyes burn for the last several hours. But she still had to get home and get the girls to bed.

During the trip home, sadness had welled up within her until it became a physical pain pressing against the walls of her chest. The pressure had been building inside of her for days, for weeks, really. Yet this weekend had pushed it to the max. Handing Joe her ring and walking away from him at the airport was the final straw. She had to let the tears come, or else she felt like she would explode. She just had to get home and get the girls to bed. Then, she could grieve for the marriage she could have had, the marriage she had given up.

"Mommy, did you hear me?" Kelsi asked, her question sweet and innocent. Jessi bit her lip. How was she supposed to tell the girls that things had changed? And what was going to happen in the coming years? She couldn't keep them from having a relationship with their father, but seeing Joe would hurt too much. How could she see him and spend time with him, all while knowing she loved him and could be married to him? Or at least she could have been if she hadn't walked away…again. The pain that was sure to wreak havoc on her heart in the coming years was her fault alone. She had once again chosen this, just as she had for the past several years. There was never anyone else to blame – no one but her.

"Yes, I did. I'm sorry, Honey. Mommy's just a little distracted tonight. I'm not sure when we'll see Daddy again." All was quiet from the backseat until Kamryn's small voice broke the silence.

"Well, I hope it's soon."

"Me too," Kelsi agreed. Jessica smiled sadly. Her girls were so sweet, so innocent, so perfectly ignorant of all the underlying currents and circumstances that were splitting their family apart, this time for good. She would have to tell them eventually, have to explain that they weren't going to get married after all, but she didn't have the energy or the emotional stability quite yet.

Her thoughts drifted to her family, and she realized she would have to tell them, too, that the wedding was off. They needed to cancel their reservations and see if they could get their money back. Jessi slumped in her seat at the thought of it. Maybe she could wait just awhile on that, too. Surely it wouldn't make a difference if they knew this week or next.

She pulled into her assigned parking place and wearily climbed out of the vehicle, unbuckling and lifting Kelsi and Kammy out of the SUV, setting them on the ground. At the rear hatch, she handed each of them something to carry, then pulled her purse up onto her shoulder, and lifted the heavy suitcase out of the back. She set it on the ground, lifted the handle, and prepared to pull it into the building.

"Come on, girls, let's head inside," she instructed, motioning for them to go ahead of her and she would follow. The twins plodded across the parking lot to the door, their shoulders drooping, but found the energy to smile at the doorman, Cliff. Jessi smiled and thanked him as well, before joining the girls at the elevator. She looked down into their tired faces as they waited for the elevator to arrive, and realized that the weekend had taken as much out of them as it had her. Of course, their reasons for being tired were different, but just as valid.

"You girls sleepy?" she asked, feathering her hand through Kelsi's hair as the elevator doors shut behind them. Her five-year-olds nodded in unison. "How about we go to bed as soon as we're done with dinner?" Jessi suggested. Again, they nodded as they followed her out of the elevator and down the hall.

They were less than five feet from their front door when Jessica realized the door was open a crack. She stopped abruptly. She knew she had checked and double-checked the door before they left for the airport. She was absolutely certain. And that meant someone had been or was in her apartment.

Fear instantly exploded within her, and she shot her hand out to stop the girls. "Girls, turn around and run back to the elevator. Push the button as many times as it takes until it opens. When it opens and you're inside, tell Mommy," she instructed as calmly and quietly as possible. She wasn't sure what she would do if someone came out of her front door, but she certainly wasn't going to turn her back while the elevator door was shut, her girls were still in the hall, and she was defenseless.

To her overwhelming relief, both girls turned and did exactly as she said. She slipped her phone out of her pocket, keeping her eyes on her front door.

"Mommy, it's ready," Kamryn told her, and Jessica left the clumsy suitcase, turned and ran to the elevator, pushing the button to close the doors until they were safely shut inside. Her heart was racing. She looked down at the girls' large, confused eyes, and couldn't find the words to explain. Instead, she put a finger up to motion for them to wait and dialed her cell phone.

When the 911 operator picked up, Jessica calmly gave her address and asked if a police officer would come over to look through her house. She explained that she had reason to believe someone was guilty of breaking and entering, and that she was standing in an elevator with her daughters and was not at liberty to say more. The kind woman on the other end of the line promised to send someone over right away, and Jessica arranged to meet them in the lobby.

Stepping out of the elevator, she looked around for Cliff, then pointed the girls toward the sitting area. She handed Kelsi her cell phone after hitting the speed dial for Jari's number. "I want you to tell Jari that she and Grandpa need to come over right away, and that I say it's very, very important. And tell her to have Grandpa contact his security. Can you remember that?" Kelsi nodded, her eyes scared and full of questions.

"I'll help her," Kamryn offered. Jessi nodded and turned to find Cliff right behind her. She jumped, her nerves on edge, but relaxed as his familiar face registered.

"Is everything alright, Miss Jessica?" he asked, his weathered face gentle and concerned. Jessica offered a shaky smile, and, taking his arm, led him away from the girls. She licked her lips in hopes that moisture would somehow return to her mouth.

"My door, my front door is open. Not just unlocked, but open, just a crack. I know I shut and locked it. I double-checked it before we left." Cliff's eyebrows drew together in worry.

"Have you called the police, Miss?"

"Yes, they should be here any minute."

"Good. I'll keep an eye on your little ones if you want, while you're with the police, or at least until your family gets here. I assume they're coming." Jessica nodded, feeling both grateful for his offer and apprehensive about leaving Kelsi and Kamryn. He winked at her. "Don't worry, Miss Jessica, I won't let anyone touch your girls. They would have to get through me first, and I'm a little tougher than I look. Fought in Vietnam back in the day and I know how to pack a pretty powerful punch, even if I've got some arthritis these days."

Jessi let out a sigh of relief, finding solace in Cliff's reassuring words that he had laced with humor. She smiled. "Thank you." Cliff nodded and hurried back to his post to open the door for the police officers who had just pulled up outside.

Two police cars, three policemen. As soon as they entered the building, Cliff pointed them to Jessica. She quickly turned to the girls. "Did you get a hold of Jari?" she asked.

Kelsi nodded. "She's on her way with Grandpa."

"Good. You girls sit here and wait. Don't move a muscle. Mr. Cliff is going to keep an eye on you, okay?" Both girls nodded and Jessica turned back to the policemen.

"Please come with me," she told them, directing them away from the girls. Her five-year-olds were hungry, tired and concerned. The last thing she wanted was to add to their alarm or cause fear before she even knew if it was warranted. If someone had indeed broken into their apartment and the girls had to be told, so be it. But Jessica wanted to have more than speculation if she was going to disrupt their sense of security.

Around the corner, she explained the situation to the police officers. They nodded their understanding, and then told her to stay put while they went upstairs. She went back around the corner to wait with the girls. She sat down, holding one of her daughters in each arm. With her first quiet moment, she felt herself filling with frustration. "Not this LORD, not now. A car accident, a broken engagement and now this?" she murmured to herself.

"Do not fear. I am close to the brokenhearted and weary. I am your refuge." The quiet words washed over her heart, and her racing pulse seemed to slow a little.

She thought of her cell phone in her pocket and longed to pull it out and call Joe. She could tell him what had happened, and in just a few hours he would be with her, holding her, protecting her. She felt vulnerable and exposed sitting on the couch with the girls. Bless his heart, Cliff wasn't going to be much of a deterrent for anyone wanting to hurt her and her kids. She would feel so much better, so much safer, if Joe was watching over them. In that moment, she began to doubt her decision from earlier more than she had in the hours since she left or the days beforehand when she had wrestled with whether or not it was the right thing to do. She didn't want to go home alone with the girls one more night, much less for the rest of her life.

"Joe isn't here, but Jesus is," she murmured, re-membering that the Great Protector was with her – the One who had protected her throughout her entire life, who would do a better job than anyone else ever could, including Joe.

"I wish Daddy was here," Kamryn whimpered.

"Me too," Kelsi agreed.

Jessi let out a long sigh and kissed each girl on the head, chiding herself for worrying her daughters. Of course they would feel her fear. Of course they would sense the danger. Of course they would long for their fa-ther. "Me three."

Bill burst through the door, not giving Cliff time to open it for him, with Jari right behind him. Jessica saw him glance around, almost franticly, and held up a hand to get his attention. He crossed the distance between them in massive strides. Jessica rose to greet them, and Bill glanced at the girls before pulling Jessica away by the arm, his face stony.

"What's going on?" he demanded. Jari looped her arm through Jessi's, her face full of concern. Jessica felt her shoulders droop, thankful she was with family.

"I don't even know if it is anything, but we got home, went upstairs, stepped out of the elevator, and were almost at our front door when I noticed it was open a crack. Not locked, not latched. I instantly felt afraid and knew something was wrong. It was just a sense, I guess. The police are upstairs now checking my apartment."

Bill shook his head. "Why? Why this? As if you didn't already have enough going on. You know, Jess, maybe it's a good thing you're moving. Maybe it'll be safer for you if you're not around me."

"What are you talking about?" Jessi asked, confused. Security had never been much of an issue for the Cordel family. She could not remember feeling afraid once, or feeling like being William Cordel's daughter made her any more of a target for those with bad intentions.

"We've been receiving a few threats lately," Jari said quietly, her voice even. "It seems as though there are a few people who are not happy about the changes your dad has made in his political career and the things he now stands for." Jessi looked from Jari to Bill, who had his hands on the back of his head, his elbows out, pacing back and forth.

"Since when? Why didn't I know about these threats?"

"You've had a lot on your plate, Jess. This is supposed to be the happiest time in your life," Jari explained. "Plus, you've been away – we didn't want to tell you over the phone."

"You shouldn't have to deal with any of this stuff," Bill nearly barked. Jessi knew his tone was not meant for her and took no offense. "None of us should. For heaven's sakes, I'm in politics, not crime."

Jessica swallowed hard, confused as to what all of it meant, afraid now that she knew that whatever had happened upstairs may involve a substantial threat. She glanced to where the girls sat, just out of earshot, and saw that Kelsi had fallen asleep on Kamryn's lap, and that the little blonde was fighting to keep her eyes open. "I have to get them to bed," she murmured.

The elevator dinged and one police officer walked out, looking grim. Jessica instantly knew that whatever he had to say wasn't good. "We'd like for you to come down to the station with us, ma'am. We need to ask you some questions."

Bill stepped closer to Jessica and put his arm around her shoulders. "I'm going, too." The officer nodded his agreement.

"I'll take the girls home and put them to bed," Jari offered, sending Jessi a sympathetic look.

Jessi wanted to protest, both for the sake of having the girls with her and knowing they were okay, and not wanting Jari to have to go home by herself after the break-in upstairs; but she looked at her sleeping five-year -olds and knew they needed to be in a bed. She nodded. "Thank you."

Bill stepped away from Jessica to hold Jari close for a brief moment and brushed a kiss against her blonde hair. "Don't worry about going home. I have security in place – you'll be safe. Get the girls to bed, and sleep soundly yourself. I'll go down to the station with Jess and then be home."

"You'll let me know if there are any updates?"

"I'll let you know as soon as I know something."

Jessica moved over to the couch and lifted Kelsi to her hip, trying not to wake her. She watched as Bill did the same with Kamryn. The last thing Jari needed on the way home was a barrage of questions. Neither of the girls woke, tired from their weekend in Michigan. Jari led the way out the door, as the policeman offered to carry the luggage.

Jessi and Bill buckled the girls into the car seats that always stayed in Jari's SUV, and Jari told the officer where to put the luggage. Then Jari gave Jessi and Bill hugs, and climbed in the driver's seat. "Let me know when you get home," Bill told her before giving her a kiss and shutting her door.

Bill watched until Jari and the girls pulled out of the parking lot, noting that a police car pulled away from the curb and followed her down the street. He turned to Jessica and the police officer, his face grim. "Shall we follow you to the station?"

The officer nodded as they were joined by another policeman, who had just arrived. "I'll lead the way, and Deputy Lindon will bring up the rear."

Jessi turned to the policemen. "There's actually a real threat to our safety?"

Deputy Lindon turned kind eyes toward her. "We feel there's reason to exercise caution."

Bill put his hand on Jessi's back and motioned toward the cars. "Let's do this then, shall we?" As he slid behind the steering wheel of Jessi's SUV, his expression was serious. "Whatever is going on, it's best to get to the station and find out so we at least know what we're dealing with." Jessica nodded, feeling frightened. She was thankful her dad was taking control of the situation.

~~~~~

Joe turned the diamond engagement ring over and over in the palm of his hand. It was stunning and exquisite, just like the girl who should be wearing it. He looked at each diamond, the clarity and brilliance of each stone. He looked at the small circular band and realized, with a half-smile, that it wouldn't even fit his pinky.

He sat back into his couch with a sigh. What good was an engagement ring if Jessica was no longer willing to wear it?

When she left the ring with him and boarded a plane back to Washington, D.C., she not only gave back the gift he had so patiently searched for and picked out, but even more importantly, she had shunned his love and removed herself from the life he had envisioned. Ever since high school, he was unable to picture his life without Jessica Cordel. No matter how he pictured it, where he pictured it, when he pictured it, one thing was always the same – he was living it with Jessi.

Well, he was somehow going to have to reprogram his mind, his view of the future. It was no longer that he couldn't find her or that it wasn't the timing of the LORD – they had been reunited and the time had come. Now, he was going to have to find a way to live life without her, because Jessica Cordel simply did not want to be a part of his future.

As that reality set in, Joe bent forward over his knees, crushing the ring in his hand as he rested his forehead against his balled fists. He did the one thing he had been fighting since Jessi left him standing at the airport that afternoon. His dreams shattered, the wedding called off; Joe wept.

~~~~~

Jessica woke up slowly, as if fighting her way out of a thick fog. Finally awake, she sat up feeling groggy and looked around. She was in her old bedroom at her dad and Jari's. It took several moments for it all to come back.

Had somebody really ransacked her apartment last night? Had there really been a threatening note left on her dining room table, clearly stating that if Senator Bill Cordel did not drop his support of the death penalty bill he was promoting, he would know how it felt to see his own family members executed? Had she really been at the police station with her dad until four in the morning, or had it all been a dream? She looked around her surroundings again and groaned. If she was at her dad and Jari's, it hadn't been a dream.

She climbed out of bed and walked to the door of the girls' adjoining room, peeking in to see if they were still sleeping. They were, so she left her room, padded down the hall, down the stairs and into the kitchen to see if Jari was up.

She was thankful she had thought to leave a message on Melinda's voicemail the night before so she wouldn't be expected at the office. Jessi was glad she would have the day to be with Jari – the one person who always added peace to any inner conflict Jessica experienced. Additionally, when Jessi had called her mom the night before, Carla had come down to the police station right away to be with her, not leaving until Bill and Jessi did. She had promised she would stop by Jari's after a hearing she had that morning, and Jessi was looking forward to her coming. Having her mom around was comforting in a way that nothing else was. When she was with Carla, Jessica knew that everything was going to be okay.

Entering the kitchen, she found Jari sitting at the table, a cup of coffee and her open Bible in front of her. Jari looked up and smiled. "Good morning." Her warm, peaceful greeting was more indicative of a calm, quiet morning with nothing unusual going on, rather than the actual circumstances. "There's coffee in the pot."

"Thanks." Jessi poured herself a cup of coffee, added a little hazelnut creamer, grabbed an almond poppyseed muffin out of a basket on the counter, and joined Jari at the table.

"I have good news," Jari immediately told her with a smile. Jessi looked up, raising her eyebrows as she took her first sip of coffee. "The police were able to match the fingerprints on the note to a set in the database, and they have the suspect in custody. Thankfully, we don't have a very brilliant enemy, and he left tracks. This morning he confessed to everything – breaking into your apartment, leaving the note, and the threats we received. While it was scary, it was short-lived," Jari offered, covering

Jessi's hand with hers.

Jessica let out a deep breath, trying to absorb the information. The man had been caught. The danger to her family was over. The police had him in custody. "Praise the LORD," Jessi breathed, taking a moment to thank her heavenly Father.

Jari's smile was quick. "Indeed. Thank You, Jesus!"

Jessica took the paper from her muffin and began to eat it slowly, washing it down with coffee as she continued to process the events of the past twelve hours, in addition to the news Jari had just shared. While she was profoundly relieved, it took awhile to comprehend it all. Jari sat quietly, letting her have the time she needed.

"So, that's that? We can carry on with life as normal?" Jessi finally asked.

"Yes, we can. I'll go over to your apartment with you later if you want, and we'll get things cleaned up for whenever you and the girls want to return. You're more than welcome to stay here for as long as you like, though. We certainly love having you."

Jessica nodded and took another bite of her muffin, chewing slowly. "So, that's really it? Last night, my apartment, the threats...it's over?" It was hard to comprehend that something that sprang up so suddenly and had been so scary, was over just as quickly.

Jari nodded, reaching out to squeeze Jessica's arm. "I'm sorry he involved you, Hon."

"Who was it?"

"His name is Marcus Moore. His son will likely receive the death penalty if the new bill your father is promoting passes next week." Jessi could feel Jari watching her face intently. "Three years ago, he attacked the police officer that arrested his son. That's how his prints were on file. He's not a hardened criminal, Jess, he's just a father who is hurting."

Jessi stared at Jari in disbelief. Was that compassion she heard in her step-mom's voice? "He broke into my apartment. He threatened to hurt my children, Jari."

The blonde woman nodded. "Yes, he did, but he didn't actually harm them, did he? It was only a threat. I'm not discrediting it, Jess, or saying that it was okay in anyway. I feel like punching him in the face for the scare he gave us. But he is facing his twenty-four-year-old son being put to death. He is hurting and scared himself and is trying to get someone's attention – someone that can stop what is about to happen."

Jessica sat silently, trying to process what had happened, trying to muster up the compassion that Jari was expressing. Finally, she sighed. Jari was right. Marcus Moore hadn't hurt her or her girls. He had been caught, was behind bars, and she was free to move on with her life.

"Has this changed Dad's stance on the bill?" Jari watched Jessica sip her coffee.

"Jess, Marcus Moore's son brutally raped and murdered two girls under the age of thirteen; behavior like that cannot be tolerated or go unpunished. It's a complicated issue, but it's a very specific bill. Your father will not change his stance. He believes it is a bill that will lead to justice for victims as well as increased safety for the general public. His duty to this country is to serve and protect."

"How does Marcus Moore not think that deserves punishment?" Jessi asked, feeling sick to her stomach at the details Jari had relayed.

"Maybe he does, but first and foremost, he's a father. He likely doesn't see a merciless criminal, but the little boy he watched grow up. While it's easy for us to see what a just punishment is, if you were his father, wouldn't you want to see him live, to be given a second chance?"

Jessica finished her muffin while digesting the latest question Jari had so calmly posed. Jessi wanted to find compassion, wanted to feel for the hurting father. But all she could think about was the instant terror she had felt the night before when she noticed her cracked door, her young daughters in the hallway beside her and no means of defense. She thought about the victims his son had murdered and about the victims' family members. She finally decided the issue was something she would have to take before the LORD. Forgiveness and compassion would likely be a process, something she would have to work through.

"Those look good. I think I'm going to have one, too. Can I get you another?" Jari asked, standing.

Jessi nodded. "They *are* good." Jari came back with the basket of muffins and the pot of coffee. When both of their cups were full, she put the pot back on the warmer and returned to her seat. Quiet settled over them for several minutes.

"Where's your ring, Jess?" Jari asked calmly, breaking the silence. Jessica looked down at her bare ring finger and cringed. In all the commotion of the night before, she had forgotten what she had done. Now, she didn't have the heart or the words to answer. She glanced up at Jari, hoping an answer would come, but let her gaze fall when it didn't. She reached for her coffee.

Jari nodded. "Why did you do it?"

Jessica felt her heart sink all over again. "I don't know how to make it work, Jari. Not right now, at least. Logistically, it just isn't feasible. We would need to get a new apartment, and we wouldn't have the money unless I simply transferred instead of quitting. But if I have to work, who's going to watch the girls? It has been such a huge blessing to have you so close and available to watch them. You have allowed me to do things that I would have never been able to do otherwise. I'm so thankful for you! But if we move to Michigan..."

"Did you talk to Joe and come to a mutual agreement, or did you just give your ring back and walk away?"

Jessica made a face. Sometimes her step-mom knew her too well. "I tried to talk to him, it just wasn't working."

"So, you…gave the ring back and left him standing at the airport?"

"Did he call you?" Jessi demanded.

Jari shook her head no. "So, I'm guessing that's what happened?"

"Jari! I didn't know what else to do!"

Jari held her hand up in a demonstration of peace. "I'm not judging you, just trying to understand the sequence of events." It was quiet for several seconds. "What if Joe quit school? Or just put it on pause for awhile?"

Jessi shook her head. "I could never let him do that. His schooling is so important. If he wants to be a pastor, he has to finish. And I want him to finish. Quitting school just isn't an option."

"So, what now, Jess?"

Jessi pressed her lips together and shrugged before answering. "Life goes on."

"As if Joe never came back into your life?" Jessi nodded. "But he did, Jess. You can't ignore that you have a young man who wants to marry you and build a life with you…he has for over half a decade."

"I want that, too," Jessi nearly moaned. "It just isn't going to work."

Jari leveled her gaze at Jessica. "You have two little girls who need a father, and they have one that adores them. Are you going to raise them as a single mom? You can absolutely do it. You're strong and smart and you'll get along just fine—"

"That's right. I will," Jessi agreed, grateful that Jari

was seeing reason.

"But how will you explain to them someday that they had a father who wanted nothing more than to be with you, with them, to be your husband and their father? How will you explain to them that they grew up in a broken home, and it wasn't even necessary – that it was a choice you made because working out a marriage seemed too hard?"

Jessi felt her temper flare. "That's not fair!"

"Hold on, I'm not finished. In addition to explaining it to your girls, how are you going to explain it to yourself – to your heart? You, Sweet Girl, are going to get lonely. Think about what it's really been like for the past six years. Think about going to bed alone, getting up alone, having dinner with the girls alone, spending your evenings after bedtime alone, going to company parties alone…is that what you want for the rest of your life?"

"Maybe I'll meet someone new!" Jessi shot back.

"Right, because you could love someone else more than you love Joe? Do you think there's someone else that's more perfectly suited for you? Do you think there's a man out there—" Jessi held up a hand to cut Jari off.

"I get the message, okay?" The silence stretched and finally she sighed. "Jari, sometimes love isn't enough. Sometimes, you start out loving someone, but it doesn't last." Jessi moved her coffee cup around in a circle on the kitchen table, watching how the creamy liquid swirled in her cup. After several moments of silence, she shrugged one shoulder. "I would rather spend my life missing Joe Colby than to get married, fall out of love, and end up bitter and divorced. I would rather never have him, but always want him, than to try and have it end up like that."

Jari sat back in her chair, speechless for several seconds. "Is this about your mom and dad?"

"No," Jessica answered immediately, frustrated.

"Are you sure?"

Jessica held Jari's eyes defensively for several moments, then threw out her hands. "Did you hear what Grandma said when I was trying on dresses? No, I know you didn't, because you were picking out my shoes. She said that Mom had been just like me when they went wedding dress shopping! Jari, my mom was in love! She was happy! She thought Dad was everything she had ever dreamed of! She didn't get married thinking their marriage would end in divorce!"

"Jess, I know marriage is hard, and that it takes work. I've been married for seven years, remember? And we both know that the first couple of years were pretty rocky. I know that sometimes it gets hard, and some marriages don't last. But do you know what else I know?"

"What?" Jessica asked hesitantly.

"Love is a decision. You are comparing the feelings you have for Joe to the feelings your mom had for your dad, and you're probably right – they're probably similar in a lot of ways. But although you look like her, you are not your mother, and Joe is certainly not your father. What will keep you together even at the point that your parents broke apart is a decision to love one another, to stay committed, to fight for your marriage, for your relationship. You know more and are in different places individually than your mom and dad were when they got married...actually than they have been up until the last couple of years. You both know that marriage is sacred, that it is a covenant, and that it is meant to last a lifetime."

Again, Jessi held Jari's eyes for several seconds. "I know what married life was like in my house growing up, and I couldn't handle things ever coming to that with Joe. I don't know if I could survive it." Tears stung Jessi's blue eyes, and she dropped them again to study the swirling motion she was making in her coffee, hiding the telltale sign from her friend.

Jari was quiet for several moments, and Jessi startled when the older woman reached across and squeezed her hand. "It is a choice, Jessica – a choice that you will have to make every day for the rest of your life. Whatever you choose comes with consequences. The good news is that the choice is yours, and you have everything – and every One – you need to choose rightly. Will you love Joe?"

"That's not even a question, Jari. I could never stop," Jessi answered, feeling miserable.

"Then what does that love look like, Jess? Because love – true, real, perfect love – casts out fear."

~~~~~

That night, once the girls were tucked into bed and Jessica could finally crawl in bed herself, the tears were almost instant. As exhausted as she was, as much as she needed sleep, her mind was racing and her heart ached.

Everything Jari had said was true. She knew that. And she knew she loved Joe. She loved him more than she even thought possible. He was the perfect man for her, the perfect husband, the perfect father for her daughters. And she had called off the wedding.

She had acted out of fear, giving room to the enemy's doubts, and she had closed a door on something that could have been truly beautiful. Her tears soaked her pillow as her heart continued it's slow, excruciating break. Despite knowing everything she did, she wasn't brave enough to reverse what she had done. She was terrified that if she said yes to Joe now, she would lose him later. And that might just be more than she could survive.

Fourteen

Joe paced the floor of his apartment, stopping to look at the sandwich and apple that sat on a plate on the kitchen table. Turning away, he started pacing again. He couldn't eat. He had barely slept. It was only by the grace of God that he hadn't ruined his GPA in the last week.

He picked up his cell phone and dialed Jessica's number again. She hadn't answered his calls since he dropped her and the girls off at the airport the Sunday before. He had left countless messages. Every time he reached her voicemail, it filled his heart with a piercing ache. It all felt so familiar. After all they had been through in the last several months with meeting randomly on the street in D.C., dinner, finding out about the girls, the car accident, the recovery, the engagement, Christmas, wedding planning – after all of that, how could they be right back where they were over six years earlier? She had walked away, shut the door on anything they could have had, and refused to communicate with him in any way…again.

He alternated between being crushed, his heart breaking all over again every time he realized she didn't want to be with him, that he meant so little to her that she could so easily walk away, and anger. He was angry that she would do this to him again; angry that she would shut him out when all he wanted was to be her husband and the girls' father; angry that he felt so hurt; angry that she wasn't even willing to talk it out with him; angry that every time their relationship became complicated, she just walked away.

She had never been willing to work anything out together; she always just went with her first instinct, which was to run. Why had he thought a marriage with her could ever work when, as soon as something got hard, she simply left?

"Why couldn't she have just talked to me about it?" Joe asked aloud, his voice angry. Surely he at least deserved that much – a conversation, a chance to talk things out. Surely he deserved more than her ring and watching her walk away.

He pulled back the kitchen chair violently and dropped into it, taking a big bite of his sandwich. Just because she walked out of his life again, taking his daughters with her, didn't mean he had to starve himself. He ate about half of his sandwich, then threw it down on his plate in disgust, losing his appetite all over again.

What had happened? He just didn't understand. When he left in January, she was as excited about the thought of marrying him as he was about marrying her. She had been, without a doubt, a woman in love. Then, by the time she arrived in Michigan, she was distant and cold, almost as if they were complete strangers. What had he done? What had he not done? He racked his brain, but couldn't think of anything.

Had she really been that worried about what they would do about a house and money? It was the only thing he could think of, but it made no sense whatsoever. Of course it was a concern. Of course it was something to talk about, to think about, to pray about. But was it a deal breaker? Especially after they had loved each other for seven years? Especially when they had children together? Surely not. Somehow something would work out. He knew that Jessi had seen the LORD work things out on her behalf before. How could she forget His sovereignty and His concern for the details now?

No matter how much he tried to sort through the mess, he simply couldn't understand. He knew she loved him. She said so right before she left. And he knew that deep down, in the deepest part of her heart, she would always love him.

She could never love another, because she had given him her heart as fully and completely as he had given his to her. So, why would she leave? Why would she break it off before she even experienced how beautiful they could make their marriage?

The answer was too obvious. She didn't trust him. She didn't trust him to provide for her, to provide for the girls. She didn't trust him to take care of them. She didn't trust him to do the things that were basic elements of a husband's job description. She didn't think he was good enough, strong enough, man enough. The realization came like a punch in the gut, just as it had so many times in the past week. She loved him all right, but in her eyes he didn't measure up.

The realization kept him from eating, from sleeping, from being able to focus on his schoolwork. It was that realization which kept him from jumping on the next plane to D.C. and convincing her to reconsider.

If she had been scared, that would have been one thing. If she had been nervous about making such a big a commitment, it would have been easier to handle. If she had forgotten who he was, and needed him to remind her, he could have done it. But not measuring up, not meeting her expectations...what could he do about that? He had always tried to be the best that he could be for her. He had always been a gentleman, always tried to be sensitive and assure her of his love for her. He had tried to be a good father, and always let her know that she and the girls were his priority, and yet, it hadn't been enough.

He pushed his cell phone away and twirled his apple by the stem until the stem broke, and the apple fell onto his plate with a thud. He sat back in his chair and let out a loud sigh. Why did loving Jessica have to be so hard? Why, when he only wanted to be with her, did she run?

Suddenly, he could hear his dad telling him that she had left as a selfless sacrifice, that she wanted him to be free to pursue his dreams, and that she hadn't wanted to hold him back. The words were ones his dad had spoken during one of their conversations the previous fall, when Joe had told his parents that they had granddaughters. Now, the memory felt like a splash of cold water. For the first time, he wondered if maybe, just maybe, Jessica was doing it again.

She had said that day at the park that she would never ask him to quit school. She wanted him to have everything he had ever dreamed of.

Suddenly, like a light bulb coming on, he understood what he'd been missing, what had driven her to call it off and walk away. He groaned as he put his head in his hands.

She wasn't the one putting pressure on herself to perform, to make it work, to provide and take care of things. She wasn't taking on his role because she thought less of him. She wasn't putting herself in the position of the one who was supposed to have it all together because she thought he wasn't enough. It wasn't her at all. The only one putting those pressures on her was him. Just as it always had been.

~~~~~

Joe sat in the library, books spread out in front of him, trying to work on his research paper; but all he could think about was how selfish he had been over the last several years. His relationship with Jessica had always been marked by his selfishness. Over and over he had put his own desires, dreams, and comfort over what was best for her.

It had started with dating her the summer they met. Looking back, he wasn't foolish enough to believe that dating her had been a mistake, but his reasoning had been wrong and selfish. He had a heart for the lost and a desire to see unbelievers know Jesus – which was a good thing. But he had agreed to date her out of selfishly thinking it would give him the opportunity to introduce her to Jesus. Additionally, he had been as attracted to her and intrigued by her in high school as he was now. As a non-Christian, she was off-limits; as a Christian, she would have been fair game – more self-serving motives. His intentions had been good, but his implementation, ulterior motives, and reasoning, wrong.

It had culminated the night he took her down to the river and got her pregnant. He never thought of what that night would mean for Jessica, or how it would affect their future. All he thought of at the moment was how he couldn't stand to think of his life without her. He couldn't bear the thought of an entire year of her being back under her father's roof and virtually, off-limits. He needed her with him, and it was the only way he thought he could make that happen.

Now, he shook his head. One night of foolish and selfish actions had cost him six years with Jessica and caused him to miss the first five years of his daughters' lives. What's more, he could never go back and do it the right way; never protect and cherish her purity; never give her the gift of starting their marriage right. Now, even if they did marry one day, they would always know they had done things out of order. Their daughters would always be at least five years older than the number of years they were married.

As it often did when he thought about the consequences of his actions that night, his stomach felt queasy. The cost of his selfishness had been very great.

Now, almost six years later, their relationship was still marked by his selfishness. He was asking Jessica and the girls to give up everything they knew, everyone they loved, to move to Michigan so *he* could finish school, so *he* could achieve *his* dream of becoming a pastor. Jessica would have to work so he could finish school. The girls would have to go to daycare with someone they didn't know so Jessica could work. He was asking Jessica, Kelsi and Kamryn to sacrifice a lot so that he could continue on as planned.

Now, he could see how selfish he had been and

wanted to change it. He wanted to transition from being selfish to selfless, yet he didn't know how. He had to finish school. He had invested so much in it already and was so close to finishing. Besides, his dream of being a pastor would build a future for them all.

Jessica had known all along, he reasoned. She knew from the very beginning what he wanted to be someday. She had always been fine with it – maybe even more protective of his dream than he was.

Joe reached out and slid the closest book in front of him, bending over it to start reading. No matter how much he wanted to abandon his selfish ways, he had to finish school. He had come too far to quit. He had already invested too much. Pastoring was what he was called to, and he had to fulfill his calling. He hoped Jessica would understand and support him in his dream, while also giving them the opportunity to work through the challenges that brought, together.

~~~~~

"Mommy?"

"Yes, Sweet Pea?" Jessica asked. She was cuddling with the girls on the couch. Her five-year-olds should already be in bed, but they had begged to be allowed to cuddle for a few minutes, and Jessi had been enjoying it too much to put an end to it.

Kelsi turned sweet green eyes up to her. "Jari says I have your mouth. Do I have your mouth?" Jessica laughed. She wasn't sure whether her friend had been referring to the physical shape of Kelsi's mouth or the blunt things that came out of it.

"I think she was right. I think you do have my mouth." Kelsi seemed satisfied, and Jessi held her a little closer. She liked that her little girl wanted to be like her.

"Jari usually is right about things," Kamryn added matter-of-factly.

"Yes, she is," Jessi agreed.

"She said Kelsi and I both have Daddy's eyes, and I

think she's right about that too. I looked at Daddy's, and his are the exact same color as ours."

Jessi nodded. "Yes, they are. They're the 'Colby eyes'. All of Daddy's sisters have them, too."

"Like Aunt Kara?" Kelsi asked.

Jessica nodded. "Yes, and look sometime – Aunt Kimberly and Aunt Kaitlynn have them too. So does Grandpa Chris."

"Next time we see them, I'm going to look," Kamryn announced, snuggling into Jessi's side.

"Me too," Kelsi added.

Jessica looked down at the two little bodies cuddled in so tightly to her own, and her heart swelled. If she didn't have the girls, she wouldn't know how deeply it was possible to love another human being. She tightened her arms around them a little more and tipped her head back against the couch in silent gratitude. *Besides Joe.* The thought startled her, yet she knew it was true. Joe had taught her the same thing, but somehow, it was different, she reasoned. She let herself settle back into silent gratitude.

She was thankful she had them; thankful they were both safe and healthy; thankful that the scare from the week before was over, and they were back in their apartment; thankful that both of her girls were little cuddlebugs; thankful that she was sitting on the couch snuggling with them, rather than in some damp school, wading through a flooded house, or digging through the rubble that used to make up someone's life. "Thank You, Jesus," she whispered under her breath.

"Mommy?"

"Yes?"

"Do you think Daddy will like to cuddle with us when you guys get married?" Kammy asked. Jessica glanced down at the dainty blonde, then up at the ceiling.

She had done a lot of thinking since her conversation with Jari and felt more confused than ever. For the past week, she felt as if the LORD had taken her to one memory after another, as well as different places in her heart where she had formed assumptions, realities and concepts about love, marriage and family, many of which had been unconscious up until that point. It was as if the LORD was inviting her to confront those hurts and misconceptions, recognize them, and let Him heal them.

She had thought of calling Joe several times, and had typed in a text message twice, just to erase it before hitting send. She wanted to talk to him, but didn't know exactly what to say or how to start. More than anything, she felt like it wasn't time. It wasn't time for her, and she had an odd sense that it wasn't time for him either. She didn't know exactly what the future held or how it would play out, but she knew the answer to Kamryn's question. "Absolutely. If Daddy were here, I know he would love to be cuddling with us."

Kelsi let out a sigh. "I hope it's May soon! It's taking a very long time to get here."

"Very long," Kamryn echoed.

Jessi counted the weeks up in her head and nearly disagreed with the girls before thinking better of it. She was supposed to marry Joe Colby in just under eight weeks. *Eight weeks.* And she had not worn his ring or talked to him for over a week. As the days slipped away, bringing them ever closer to May, that knowledge was overwhelming to her and more than a little scary. However, Jari had refused to call the resort and cancel just yet. She said they could cancel up until the fifteenth of April, and she wanted to give Joe and Jessi time to think…and talk.

"What's this?" Jessi asked, lifting Kelsi's hand and rubbing at a spot of pink in the wrinkle of her knuckle.

"What?" Kelsi asked, leaning forward to look at her hand. "Oh, we made handprints today. Mine was pink."

"Mine was purple," Kamryn interrupted.

"Miss Susan said we can bring them home tomorrow.

They had to dry overnight," Kelsi explained.

"We made them on clay. Miss Susan says they can be used as a hot pad," Kamryn added.

"Huh. A hot pad, you say? I just happen to need two more hot pads. I don't have very many," Jessi answered. "I am very excited to see them, and we'll use them to put our pots on tomorrow for dinner." Both girls beamed.

Jessica glanced up at the clock. "Oh girls! It's almost nine o'clock – almost an hour past your bedtime! Run into bed, okay?" Reluctantly, the girls obeyed, climbing off the couch and running into the bathroom one last time before bed. Jessica stood slowly and stretched before following. She was as reluctant to put them to bed as they were to go, because after they were in bed, she would be alone, just as she was every night. She thought longingly about how nice it would be if Joe were there to help her put them to bed. Then they could relax, watch a movie, read a book, or just cuddle on the couch.

"Mommy, I told Kamryn I had to go potty *really* bad, but she wouldn't let me go first!" Kelsi cried in outrage, stomping out of the bathroom. Jessica looked at the little brunette in the long nightgown, her arms crossed and her eyebrows drawn together, and had to put effort into hiding a grin. She started across the room toward her. "I thought it would be unselfish of her to let me go first since I had to go *really* bad, but no! She wouldn't let me!" Kelsi tattled.

"It was my night to go first!" Kamryn cried from the toilet. Jessica bent down and scooped Kelsi up in her arms, tickling her. Her tickling drew shrieks of laughter from the little girl as Jessi carried her into the bathroom.

"Alright, alright, little Miss. This isn't worth a fight. You done, Kam?" Jessica asked, rounding the corner into the bathroom.

Kamryn was just flushing. "Yes!"

"Good. Your turn, Kels."

~~~~

"God, I can't give it up," he stated matter-of-factly.

"Choose my ways." The quiet whisper that seemed to echo around him not only stunned but frustrated Joe.

"What do you mean choose Your way? This *is* Your way! Sacrificing it all for the sake of the ministry, for the sake of seeing the lost come to You. Isn't that what You want? Isn't that Your way?"

"The lost are in the world, Son."

"And in the church."

"And in the world."

Joe shook his head in frustration. "You are the One, God – You're the One who gave me this dream of being a pastor. You're the One that called me to it. I know You did. I know You've called me to pastor!"

"Pastor the flock I give you."

"So, You sent me down this road, had me waste years of my life, only to change direction now?"

"I do not waste. I work in mysterious ways. Choose my ways."

Joe let out a sigh so deep he felt as if he had been holding it for days. He ventured to ask the question he was most nervous to have answered. "What are Your ways?"

"I do not waste. I gave you a gift, Joe, a talent. Do what you were made to do, and I will bring your flock."

"What was I made to do?" Joe asked, searching his mind. There were several things the LORD had given him success in. Which was he supposed to pursue?

"You'll be in full-time ministry. I have called you to it, but it won't be what you expect. Watch for it."

"Watch for it," Joe repeated to himself. He mulled over the conversation in his mind for several moments. "What do I do about school? Do I finish?" There was no answer. Joe asked the question again. Still, no answer.

As if fighting his way through a fog, Joe woke slowly and blinked several times. Suddenly, he sat up in bed and looked around. Had he been dreaming? Had the conversation he just had with the strong, quiet Whisper been a dream, or had it been real? He rubbed his eyes and looked around again. "What do I do about school?" he asked into the stillness of his dark bedroom. He waited, but heard nothing. Uncertain as to the next step he should take, he lay back down, and his eyes fell on the blue neon numbers of his clock. They read five twenty-five a.m. He closed his eyes and sighed. He had to get up in an hour and five minutes.

Randomly he saw, 'Ephesians 5:25', scroll across the screen of his mind and, curious, he sat up and grabbed his Bible off his bedside table. He knew what Ephesians five was about, and it seemed a most unhelpful passage for the question he had just posed, the conversation he had just had, and his lingering questions about direction. Still, he knew the Word was living and felt expectation begin to build as he thumbed through the worn pages until he reached the correct passage.

"Husbands, love your wives, just as Christ also loved the church and gave Himself for her," he read aloud, and then continued. "That He might sanctify and cleanse her with the washing of water by the Word, that He might present her to Himself a glorious church, not having spot or wrinkle or any such thing, but that she should be holy and without blemish. So husbands ought to love their own wives as their own bodies; he who loves his wife, loves himself. For no one ever hated his own flesh; but nourishes and cherishes it; just as the LORD does the church."

Joe scooted back to lean against his headboard, stretching his legs out and leaving his Bible open in his lap. He read through the passage again, then leaned his head back and closed his eyes, letting his mind connect the dots.

It didn't matter that he wasn't legally married. It didn't matter that she no longer wore his engagement ring. In his heart and mind, he had been married to Jessica Cordel for over half a decade. That wouldn't change no matter what happened in the next ten or twenty years. He was committed to her. He would stay faithful to her. He loved her...but what had He given for her? The question hit him like a ton of bricks. If He was to be to her as Jesus was to the church, then what had he given? What had he laid down? Had he cherished her? Nourished her? Cared for her?

His stomach churned as he realized the truth. She had given up her youth, her freedom, to have and raise his children. She had given up his support, help and love, so that he could achieve his dreams. She had learned to survive on her own as a working mother, played the role of mom, dad, provider, caretaker, nurse, taxi driver, teacher and every other role commonly shared by both parents, all so he could have everything he ever wanted. Now, she was giving up the life he knew she wanted with him, so he wouldn't have to give up his schooling or his career.

She was right. There was no way their family could make it if he was going to school full-time, and she was working full-time in Michigan. The biggest issue was childcare, because if she had to work, it meant she would be gone for days, maybe weeks or a month at a time. Without Jari, Carla, or Maybelle, there wasn't anyone they knew or trusted enough to leave their girls with.

And so, once again, instead of asking him to sacrifice anything for the sake of her and the girls, Jessica took the burden on herself. She sacrificed her own happiness, her own comfort. She cut the unavoidable discrepancy brought by reality out of the cloth of her own dreams and desires, and did the one thing that would allow him to continue on the course he had set for himself. She left. Again.

One question echoed in every chamber of his heart and mind. *What had he sacrificed for Jessica?*

What had he laid down? What had he given up? How had he been a representation to her of Christ with the church? Had he ever been the one to make up for the lack? Had he ever been the one to suffer for her sake? Had he loved her as he loved himself? Had he put her needs above his own, nourished her, cared for her, provided for her as he had himself?

He always rationalized his selfishness by reminding himself that his course was one the God of Heaven had laid out for him. He couldn't say no to the LORD for the sake of any girl, even if he truly loved her. He couldn't deny what he was meant to do. But maybe, if the conversation in his dream had been real, maybe the course the LORD had put before him was changing, taking an unexpected turn. Maybe he had been clinging so tightly to where he thought the path was going, based on where it had started, that he missed the sharp curve that was taking him somewhere else. Maybe following Jesus in this season of his life meant laying down his life for another – for his bride.

He sprang out of bed and headed to the shower, ready to start his day with enthusiasm. In the quiet morning hours, he had not only taken part in one of the most real conversations with God that he had ever had, but two things had become crystal clear. It was time for him to step up into the position of the head of his family and love them with a sacrificial love as Christ loved the church, and it was time for him to figure out what came after the end of spring semester, because next fall, he wasn't going back to school.

Fifteen

Joe leaned back in his chair, crossing his arms over his chest, hoping the added barrier would aid in keeping his fellow students from hearing how his belly growled with hunger. The food one of the teachers was warming up in the break room down the hall was creating a heavenly aroma that drifted in the open classroom door and reminded his stomach he hadn't eaten in three days. Still, he needed answers, direction and wisdom, and he would fast until the LORD gave clarity.

He was in no way interested in attempting to manipulate God into speaking, but simply desired to be more aware, alert and watchful in his weakened and desperate state. If the prophets, kings and disciples of old could fast, he could, too.

Since his morning of revelation three days earlier, he had been asking for mercy. Even though he had made a mess of things, he was asking that God, in His great mercy, would not give him what he deserved, but make a way for things to be made right. He wanted a wife. He wanted a family. He wanted to be doing whatever it was he was created to do. And he wanted to be in a physical state that would open his senses to watch for how the LORD was going to move. Dragging his thoughts from his circumstances and hunger, he refocused on the professor in front of him.

"Did God require a sacrifice of Abraham?" the professor was asking. "Yes. But He provided for the sacrifice out of His own abundance. God was never interested in Abraham sacrificing his son. He was interested in Abraham's heart, in his trust. He had given Abraham a promise, and He wanted to know – and wanted Abraham to know – if Abraham would trust Him to bring the promise about, even if it looked like the only route to the fulfillment of that promise was about to die on a stone altar. But what did Abraham do? He had such a deep relationship with God, he had learned to trust him so deeply during their years together in Canaan, that he had committed in his heart that he would be obedient because he knew God was faithful. If he sacrificed Isaac, he knew God was powerful enough to raise him from the dead to fulfill His promise or do *something* to fulfill the promise that he would be the father of many nations. Abraham was a man who was *confident* in the faithfulness of God. He was a man who, in his heart, sacrificed the logical route to the end result in favor of God's route, because time and experience had proven to him that God's route was always better.

"After all, remember what had happened years earlier, when he and Sarah tried their own way of producing a son that would make Abraham the father of many nations?" the professor continued. "All they succeeded in doing was creating a huge rift within their household.

"So, here we have Abraham, full of trust and faith, marching up the mountain with Isaac, knowing full well he might be descending the mountain alone." The professor grabbed a quick breath before plowing ahead. "He builds the altar, positions the wood, binds Isaac, lays him on the altar and picks up his knife. Now look at this, chapter twenty-two verse eleven – the angel of the LORD calls out to Abraham and what? He stops him and shows him that the LORD has changed the plans and provided a different sacrifice than Isaac. But what would have happened if Abraham had been so focused on what the LORD said in the beginning, that he missed the curveball that had been thrown to save the life of his son? What if he had been so legalistic, like many of us, that he said, 'No, the LORD said to sacrifice Isaac, and that's what I'm going to do no matter what.'

"This is why we have to be so sensitive to the Holy Spirit! God does not change – He is the same yesterday, today and forever; however, sometimes He sends us out in one direction only to change it and take us somewhere completely different. It's not that His plans change, that He changes His mind, or finds a better way. He knew there was going to be a ram sacrificed that day all along, but Abraham needed to make the journey. I believe he was a different person – that he went to a new level in his walk with the LORD – because of the walk he made up the mountain with Isaac.

"But imagine if he hadn't been sensitive to the voice of the LORD and hadn't heeded it. If he had gone through with killing Isaac, his son would be dead, and that was never part of the plan. Is God big enough to have fixed the situation should Abraham have actually killed Isaac? Yes, I believe He is. But it wouldn't have been the best. Isaac dying was never in the plan, only Abraham being willing to lay down his own will for God's and trust that when all seemed lost, God had a plan to fulfill the promise."

The professor glanced at the clock and groaned. "Time's up already and we're just getting to the good part. Tomorrow, we'll look at how God demonstrates His heart and uses Abraham and Isaac as a prophetic picture of Jesus. I posted the exam grades online, so you can check those out, and I'll hand your exams back on Thursday. See you tomorrow."

Joe sat for several seconds without moving, trying to absorb everything the man in front of him had just said. It felt so significant, so pertinent to his own situation. He let out a deep breath. "The Living Word," he breathed quietly before closing his notebook and Bible, then turning to put them in his bag.

"Hey Joe, you play any football these days?" Joe glanced up at the middle-aged classmate who had stopped beside him.

"Not much, Tony," Joe admitted, rubbing the back of his neck. "Sometimes I throw one around with the guys but that's about it."

"Too bad. I watched you play when you were in college, and you were made to play the game. You should do that as long as your body will allow."

Joe looked up sharply. "What did you say?" Tony studied Joe for several seconds as if worried he had offended him. Joe held up a hand to disarm him. "It's just how you said it...it...it just...I think someone else said something very similar," he stammered.

His classmate shrugged. "Oh, well it's true. Watching you play, watching you throw...you were made to play football."

Joe nodded slowly. "Maybe I was."

Joe mulled over Tony's off-handed comment the rest of the day, along with the lecture on Abraham. He wanted to think it was simply a coincidence, but it felt like it fit. He felt a peace settle deep within him that he hadn't felt since even before his conversation with Jessica, before she left, before his early morning encounter with Truth.

When he got home that night, he made a beeline to the dresser that served as his computer desk and opened the top drawer, searching through sticky notes and business cards until he found the one he sought. He dialed the number and chatted for a few minutes before getting to his reason for the call. As a result, he set up an appointment for the following Saturday afternoon. When he hung up, he got online and, after checking his bank account, purchased a ticket from Grand Rapids to Minneapolis.

As he printed his e-ticket, he took a deep breath to steady himself. Everything was unfolding – or unraveling – so quickly. Less than two weeks ago he had been engaged to be married, with a career as a pastor not more than a year or two down the road. Finishing seminary was the only thing standing between him and his occupational dream. Now, the wedding was called off, he had no fiancé, and he was planning to quit school after the end of semester. In just a few days he was flying to Minneapolis to meet with the offensive coach of Minnesota's pro football team to see if he could play ball for him next season.

He took another deep breath and rubbed his palms back and forth on the legs of his jeans. The funny thing was that he had more peace now, in the midst of the unknown, things looking completely different than he had ever pictured, than he had when he thought he could predict the next five years, if not ten.

He thought about calling Jessica and telling her of his decision, but decided against it. The next several steps had to be taken in the correct order. He needed to meet with the coach and see where that possibility might lead before talking to Jessi. At this point, he still had nothing to offer, nothing to promise, and he needed to have something by the time he talked to her. If he was going to ask her to leave her family, her job, her home and the life she had built for herself and the girls over the past six years, he better have something to offer, something for her to come to. He wanted her to know that she would be taken care of. For once, he wanted to give her the chance to dream.

~~~~~

"Your call last week threw me for a loop, Colby," Bob Gingrite told Joe after taking his seat at the tall table Joe had been sitting at when the offensive coach walked into the restaurant. The man, in his mid-sixties with graying hair around his temples, shook his head. "I never would have guessed it. College star gets an offer to play in the big leagues, turns it down to go to seminary only to call out of the blue two years later and asks to meet for lunch. What's next, Joe?"

Joe grinned. "I want to play ball." He knew Coach Gingrite might laugh in his face – there were likely hundreds of guys who wanted to play football for him. There was a process for playing in the league, and Joe wasn't following any of it. The team surely already had their roster pretty well settled.

To his credit, the older man didn't laugh, but simply nodded. "I figured that's why you wanted to meet."

Joe leaned forward in his seat, resting his forearms on the table. "I know I've been out of the game for quite awhile, and I know I have a lot of work to do to get back into playing condition – and even more to play professional football. I get that. I know you just drafted Ryans, and that I certainly wouldn't be starting. But Coach, you believed in me two years ago, enough to ask me to join your team and eventually lead it – hopefully to some superbowl titles – and I'm asking you to believe in me again. Let me come to spring training, let me practice with you through the summer, and I'll prove to you that I'm still a man you want on your team."

Bob Gingrite leaned back in his chair and rubbed his jaw with his large hand, studying Joe. Rather than answer, he finally picked up a menu. "Got to say, this is one of my favorite places. You ever had their reuben? You don't find a reuben like theirs just anywhere." Joe shook his head and picked up his menu, too, silently agreeing to let the man have some time to think. The waitress came.

"I'm going to have a reuben with fries and an iced tea," Bob told the girl standing beside him, handing her his menu.

"I'll have the same," Joe told her with a grin, handing her his menu as well.

Bob folded his hands on the table. "So, Colby, what have you been up to for the past two years? You going to school? Have you found yourself a woman yet?"

Joe dipped his head in a quick nod. "Yes, sir. Both."

"Well, good for you. A man doesn't truly know who he is until he has his woman beside him," Bob paused. "My wife, Laura, and I just celebrated forty years. Best forty years of my life."

Joe grinned. "That's great, Coach. Congratulations."

"Yeah, our kids took us on a cruise down to the Caribbean to celebrate. Prettiest water I've ever seen down there. Wouldn't let me throw a line over the back of the boat, though, so not much in the way of fishing; but we went on one of them fishing excursions, they call it, and I pulled in a real good-sized shark. The wife wanted to go snorkeling the next day, but I wasn't real keen on getting in the same water I'd just pulled him outta the day before. You know what I'm saying?"

Joe nodded. "Makes sense."

"Oh, but my grandkids sure enjoyed the boat. We've got twelve of 'em and they were running around the ship, swimming in the pool, going down the slides and eating the ice cream day and night. In the airplane on the way back, Kurt's youngest, Izzy, was sitting beside Grandma and asked, 'Nama, can you and Papa have another fortieth anniversary again soon?' Ain't that just precious?"

Joe nodded again. "Sounds like she enjoyed herself."

"She did. They all did," Bob paused as the waitress set their drinks down in front of them. "Thank you, ma'am." He proceeded to empty three sugar packets into his drink and stir it emphatically.

"You know, everyday, Colby, you know the first thing that crosses my mind?" Joe shook his head. "I thank God that my heart's still beating, that I get another day on His green earth. Then I turn my head and thank Him that I wake up beside the most beautiful woman in the world. She sure keeps getting better with time, and LORD knows I don't, so she's put up with a lot over the years." Joe smiled at the tender tone the Coach's voice took on as he spoke of his wife. "Say, Son, when are you getting married? You said you'd found a girl, but you're not wearing a ring. Didn't figure you to be like a lot of these guys who avoid marriage at all costs to keep their options open. Let me tell you, if you've found a good girl that you love and she loves you back, that's the best option you've got."

"The wedding is set for this May."

"Ah, not too far off, then, huh?"

"No sir."

"Well, you enjoy every moment of it. It goes way too fast."

"I will. I sure will," Joe answered with another grin.

The waitress returned with their meals. "Didn't I tell you their reuben was something else? Just look at that." Joe nodded, having to admit that the sandwich looked amazing. It was a fitting meal to break his fast with. He reached for his sandwich and took his first bite with gusto.

They ate in silence for several minutes until both of their sandwiches were gone, and they had a good start on their fries. Joe waited patiently. "I appreciate a man who will let another man eat in peace," Bob finally said, reaching for more ketchup.

"My dad often said that some things just don't mix, and conversation and a good meal are two of them," Joe answered with a grin. Chris Colby may have joked about that often enough, but the whole family knew that mealtime at the Colby house was a time for conversing.

"Wise man," Bob agreed with a chuckle. "Wish he could explain that to my wife. She sure does like to talk during a meal. She'll still be finishing her food an hour after the rest of us are done because she's been so busy chitchatting. She'll talk so long, her food will be absolutely cold by the time she gets around to eating it. Now tell me, what is the point of that?"

Joe grinned, thinking of his mom and her similar behavior. "Women will be women."

"Ah, and you gotta love 'em, all their chitchatting and all." Bob finished his last fry. "Here's the deal, Colby. I can't give you a spot on the team, just like that. I'd like to, I really would. I think you're a great guy, and you showed a whole boat-load of protential back in college. But the truth is, you haven't played competitive ball in two years, and we're talking about the pros here, not the YMCA league."

Joe nodded, trying to keep up with the sudden change in conversation.

"But I want you to work your butt off, come to spring training, come practice with us this summer, and we'll see what happens at the start of the season," Bob continued. "I'm not going to make you any promises, but if you can get back in shape, and if you can show us the same Joe Colby we saw in your college years...well, then we'll talk.

Joe nodded, grinning. "That sounds fair, Coach. All I'm asking for is a shot."

The coach considered him for several more moments before bobbing his head. "Well, you've got it, Son. You've got your second chance. Now what are you going to make out of it?"

Sixteen

Jessica was shocked when she picked up her ringing phone and saw Joe's number. He hadn't tried to call in over two weeks.

"Answer the phone. It's time." The gentle whisper blew across her heart, and without hesitation she answered. "Hey."

"Jess," he sounded both shocked and relieved that she had answered. She thought the conversation might be awkward, and began to try to formulate some sort of an explanation in her mind, but Joe kept talking. "Do you have plans this weekend?"

"No," she answered, surprised.

"Good. I'm going to send you a plane ticket. Please come."

He sounded neither hurt nor angry. There was no accusation, condemnation or guilt in his voice, only peaceful confidence. Jessica felt her heart warming, felt herself being drawn to him just as she always had been. This part of him – this part that was always confident, peaceful, and ready to move on – had always been terribly attractive, set him apart from the crowd, and had been somewhat like quicksand to her heart. She felt herself getting sucked in again.

"Jess, class is starting. I have to go, but check your email, and…please come."

"Wha—" she started.

"There'll be time for questions and conversations once we're together face-to-face. For now, just come. Please. I have to go. See you soon. I love you."

Jessi hung up her phone as she realized he was gone. She turned her chair from her office window back to her desk and put her phone down, trying to make sense of the conversation, if one could even call it that. She sat still for several seconds, then pulled up her personal email on her computer. Sure enough, there was an e-ticket in her inbox. She opened it and was confused when she saw the destination was not Grand Rapids but Minneapolis, Minnesota – a city she had never been to and had no presumable reason to visit now. She grabbed her cell phone to send Joe a quick text. 'I think there's been a mistake. This ticket is to Minneapolis.' His reply came back just seconds later. 'No mistake. Please come.'

Jessi sat back in her chair and blew out a deep breath. She had no idea what Joe Colby was thinking, or what he had planned. She was confused by the destination. She dreaded having a conversation about what she had done in Michigan and what came next for them. However, one thing was certain – if Joe Colby was asking her to fly across the country, she would. No questions asked.

~~~~~

Jessi stepped off the plane, pulling her carry-on luggage, her purse hanging from her shoulder, and her coat draped over her arm. It may be spring in D.C., but as she had seen from the airplane window, it was still very much winter in Minnesota. She looked around expectantly, assuming Joe would be waiting for her. He was.

He was crossing the distance between them with long, purposeful strides. The intensity in his expression took her breath away. She rocked back a step, trying to create some semblance of space; but he was there, embracing her, enveloping her, the smell of his cologne engulfing her. His presence was stealing her away into a million memories. Helpless to do anything else, she found herself wrapping her arms around his thick waist and holding on, pressing her cheek against his chest. It felt good to be in his arms again.

After what felt like a long time, he stepped back and held her at arm's length, grinning. "You look great, Jess. As always."

She smiled. "So do you, Joe." He took her suitcase from her and took her hand.

"Come on, we have plans."

She looked at him curiously. "Do we?" He nodded, still grinning. "What kind of plans?"

"You'll see," he told her.

As she walked along beside him, her hand snuggly in his, she tried to make sense of what was going on. The entire flight she had tried to figure out what could have caused him to fly her to Minneapolis. She had stewed about what would happen once she arrived. She wondered if he would demand an explanation, plead with her, or insist she put her engagement ring back on. Despite all of her contemplating, she had never considered this – he acted as if nothing were wrong. Additionally, she hadn't anticipated the rush to leave the airport to get to whatever he had planned.

"How was your flight, Jess?" he asked, interrupting her thoughts.

"It was fine. I'm just…I'm just confused." He grinned as they stopped in the baggage claim area.

"Here's where your bags should be," he told her, pointing to a carousel not far away. "Why don't you wait for them, and I'll run over and get mine. I just landed, too." When Jessi agreed, Joe left her to get his own luggage. He was back before the luggage from her flight ever appeared.

They were both quiet as they waited for her luggage to come, and Joe kept his distance. She shot a sideways glance at him once or twice, but he seemed intent on watching the luggage that was now moving past them on the conveyor belt. "There. That's mine," Jessi finally said, pointing at the dark luggage with the silk scarf tied around the handle. Joe had already spotted it and was on his way. He lugged her suitcase off the carousel and carried it through the crowd to her. He was trying to hide his amusement as he set it down beside her. "What?" she asked, bristling.

"How long were you planning on staying?" he joked. She made a face at him.

"You sent me a ticket to Minneapolis. I have no idea what we're doing here...I had to come prepared," she paused. "Besides, you have the same amount of luggage as I do."

"I'm staying longer," he offered simply.

That surprised her. "You are? Why?"

"I'll tell you later."

Jessica let that settle, then offered an olive branch. "I'll have you know, the whole suitcase isn't for me. The girls sent you something."

Jessica's heart ached as the tenderest expression she had ever seen filled Joe's face. "Did they? How are they?"

Jessi averted her gaze, feeling guilty for keeping Joe away from the girls for the past few weeks. When she hadn't answered his calls, it had meant no goodnight phone calls, no stories that left the girls giggling, no promises that he would be with them again soon. "They miss you."

"It's mutual," Joe answered simply, strapping their luggage together. Jessica walked with him to the car rental desk, then waited as he finalized arrangements, put their luggage in the car and helped her in. Once they were out of the airport and driving through the city, she ventured another question.

"Where are we going?"

Joe grinned. "To our hotel."

"Where are we going after that?" she asked.

"We're not going anywhere. We're staying in."

"We're staying at the hotel?" she asked, surprised. What kind of plans brought them both to Minnesota and took place in a hotel? A conference? Perhaps even a marriage conference? "What are we going to do at the hotel?"

"You'll see." Jessica bit her lip, knowing Joe had divulged as much information as he was going to for the time being. Curiosity ate at her as they finished the drive in silence. When he pulled into the hotel parking lot, she followed him to the back of the car and watched as he unloaded their luggage, locked the car, and led her inside.

At the front desk, he checked in and handed her a room key. "You're in room 305, I'm in room 306." She accepted the key and summoned the elevator. Once on the third floor, he left his luggage in the hall to take hers into her room, then walked back to the threshold. With one hand on the door, one foot in the hall, he turned back and grinned at her. "Get freshened up, call the girls, take a quick nap, whatever you want to do; but come to my room in forty-five minutes. Deal?"

Jessica cocked her head and smiled, completely confused and yet enjoying the way he was leading her step-by-step. "What should I wear?"

"Something comfortable – we'll be there for awhile," he answered with a cheerful grin. With that, he shut her door behind him, and she was left alone.

Shaking her head, she pulled out her cell phone and called Jari, filling her in on what little she knew about the mystery weekend, then talked to each of the girls. When the phone call ended, she called her mom to do the same. Then, she touched up her makeup and logged into her work email to make sure she hadn't received anything urgent. By the time she was finished, forty-three minutes had passed, so she checked her reflection, put on a bit more perfume and headed next door. She smoothed her hand over the front of her cardigan sweater, hoping to still the butterflies in her stomach, then knocked on Joe's door.

For just a moment, she was fifteen and back at Glendale's 7-Eleven, seeing him for the first time, drawn by his electric green eyes and the mystery and confidence he exuded. He swung open the door to his hotel room and for just a moment, her breath caught. His eyes were still electric, his tan was flawless, his looks striking, and still, after all these years, he exuded mystery and confidence. Even knowing his heart was hers, even knowing more about him than any other human being on the planet, he was still a mystery, still compelling. The man in front of her was not a stranger; he wasn't a man she didn't know if she could trust; he wasn't someone she had to protect her heart from. He was Joe.

He was the one who had stolen her heart, the one who had awakened her to love. He had taught her the meaning of love, belonging, and family. He was the one who had given her the most magical year of her life and the two most precious gifts she had ever been given. In that instant she knew what she had known in high school. Marriage to Joe Colby would be different than what she had seen modeled within her own family. Jari had been right. Joe wasn't her father, and she wasn't her mother. Marriage to him would be beautiful.

Jessica's heart swelled, and she wanted to reach out to him, but he swung the door open wide and stepped back. A happy grin replaced the brief expression of pure intensity, longing and hopefulness that had decidedly marked his handsome features when the door first opened. "You're right on time!" he told her as he stepped back to let her enter.

She glanced around the room and noticed the pizza on the dresser, the thick newspaper beside it, the calculator, some sort of bank statement, a pen, notepad and two cans of soda on the floor.

Joe held out his hands, motioning to what was laid out. "Welcome to our plans for this evening!"

Jessica tilted her head at him in question, a small, confused smile on her face. "I...I don't understand. What are we doing?"

Joe's grin faded, and his expression turned serious. "There have been some changes, and I need to tell you about them. Sit down. Let me get you a slice of pizza."

Jessica did as she was told, picking a spot on the floor where she could lean back against the bed. Fear pricked her heart as her imagination ran wild, fueled by Joe's words and the look on his face. What had changed? What did that mean? She tried to still her mind against the numerous what ifs that loomed.

Obviously unaware of the questions his statement had created, he turned back to her, offering a slice of pizza on a napkin and a soda. She accepted it, and waited until he sat down beside her, his back against the bed, his pizza on a napkin beside him. Joe bowed his head and offered thanks to God – thanks for bringing them both there safely, for the plans He had for them, for the doors He was opening, and for the girls that were waiting for them at home. When he said amen, and they opened their eyes, Jessica took a bite of pizza, forcing herself to allow him to lead the conversation rather than demanding answers and jumping to conclusions.

He took two bites of pizza, chewing thoughtfully and then started abruptly. "I'm not going back to school next fall." Jessica nearly choked on the drink she had just taken. She turned to him, completely caught off-guard.

"What? But—"

Joe turned so he could see her face and he met her eyes. He gave a slight shake of his head, and she let the arguments die on her lips. "I'm not going back to school, Jess. When I finish next month, I'm done. For now at least. If the LORD brings it back up at some point in the future, well then, we'll see, but for now, this is my last semester."

The finality of his tone let her know that there was no arguing. The topic was not up for discussion. "Why?" she asked, trying to recover from her shock.

His smile was tender. "Because sometimes the direction you think you're supposed to go in, only gets you to a curve in the road that takes you in an entirely new direction," he paused. "And that new direction you never would have thought you were supposed to go in, is actually better than the direction you started out going in the first place."

She shook her head. "I don't understand. I mean, I understand what you're saying, and yes, I think you're absolutely right, but what does that mean for you? Which direction are you going in now?"

Joe grinned. "I'm going to practice with Minnesota's football team next week. And I'm probably going to get my butt kicked, but I'm going to practice. Then I'm going to go home and hit the gym even harder than I have been for the past two weeks and I'm going to train. This summer, I'm going to live up here and hopefully, if Coach thinks I'm good enough and ready…well, hopefully he'll sign me, and I'll play pro ball next fall."

Jessica's mind was reeling. "You're moving to Minnesota?" Joe nodded. "You're going to play football again?"

Joe's grin was quick. "Hopefully!"

"But you said no – you turned them down when they wanted to draft you."

"A lot has happened in two years, Jess."

She shook her head. "You can't put your dreams on hold for us, Joe. I won't let you. You are supposed to be a pastor, and I'm not going to let an…an accidental pregnancy and guilt keep you from that," Jessi told him, letting out a deep breath, shifting her eyes down to her pizza. She was startled when he gently gripped her chin and tilted her face back up toward him.

"The lost are in the world as well as in the church," he told her, his entire countenance saturated in peace – a peace that, to her, felt a million miles away at the moment. "I will pastor the flock that the LORD gives me. I will look for it and wait for it while doing what I was made to do."

Joe shifted positions to face her squarely. "A few weeks ago, I'm not sure if I was awake or asleep, but I had a conversation with God, and realized He was changing my direction. He made it clear that I was to pastor – that it's my calling – but to pursue that educationally and vocationally would simply be me trying to fit my calling into the logical path. But His ways are different than our ways, Jess, and a church congregation is not the flock I'll pastor...at least not for now. He kept saying that the lost are in the world, and if I do what I'm made to do, He'll bring the lost.

"I wasn't sure what He meant or what it is that I'm made to do, so I started fasting and asking for direction. Then, one day I was sitting in class, and the professor was speaking on the story of Abraham and Isaac and I knew the LORD was moving through it in my heart. After class, a classmate made the off-handed comment that I was made to play football. He wasn't being serious or trying to change the course of my life or anything, but I knew, Jess – I just knew he was right. That's what I'm supposed to be doing right now." Joe shrugged.

"I went home and found Coach Gingrite's business card. When I was in college, Coach took me out for a few meals, and we talked a lot. When I turned down his offer to play for him, he respected my decision and said if I changed my mind, to let him know...well, I did. I flew out here two weeks ago and met him for lunch. I told him I wanted to play ball for him. He said to come back out for spring training and then train with them this summer. Jess, he couldn't make me any promises. I'm certainly not guaranteed a spot on the team, but if I can get back in shape and get my arm in shape, well, he said we would talk about it."

"Wow," Jessica breathed, studying Joe's face, trying to absorb everything he had just said.

"Like I said, I'm not guaranteed a spot on the team. Leaving your job and your family and moving to Minnesota is going to be a risk – for you, for the girls, and for me. We have nothing concrete, Jess. But I've been careful and saved up some money through college. It's not a lot, but I have seven thousand dollars in the bank." Joe grinned and held out a bank statement. "And twenty-nine cents. I have very few bills other than living expenses, and from past conversations, I think it's about the same for you. It's not a lot, but what I have is enough to rent something from May through the end of summer. I guess we'll see what happens then. If I get a spot on the team, we'll have enough to buy a house, and you can stay home with the girls. If I don't, well, I have a degree. I'll get a job and we'll make it work. Either way, LORD willing, I'll provide for our family."

Joe paused as he reached out and put his hand against her cheek. "I know it's not a fool-proof, black and white, take it to the bank kind of plan, but I really feel like I'm going to get on the team. Even if I don't, Jess, I'll figure out something. I'll do whatever it takes to provide for you and the girls, and provide enough that you can stay home with them. We won't have to leave them with someone we don't know for days and weeks at a time so you can do your job. I want your job to be whatever you want it to be, whatever you feel like it should be. Stay home with the girls, volunteer at a soup kitchen, take up sewing – whatever you want to do."

Jessica felt tears prick her eyes as what he was saying sunk in. "You would give up everything you've ever wanted for us?"

Joe tilted his head as he studied her, stroking her cheek with his thumb. "Jessica, you *are* everything I've ever wanted. You and the girls. I want to be in God's will, I want to be married to you and be a father to our children. If I have that, nothing else matters. If I have that, I have everything I need or want." Jessica blinked back tears as she let his words drench her parched heart.

For so long, she had wanted him to follow his dreams. She hadn't wanted him to sacrifice anything for her, or be held back; but now, in light of everything he had told her, she realized that the very thing she had always tried to keep him from – his sacrifice – meant everything to her.

He reached in his pocket and held his fist out in front of him. "I know it's a risk. I know it's still scary and there are no absolutes. But now you know everything. You know my plans, my hopes, my dreams and I'm wondering…" He turned his fist over and opened it to reveal her engagement ring. "Will you still marry me in May?"

His face was so hopeful, his expression so serious that it pulled on every heartstring she had. He had put himself out there and made himself vulnerable. He had sacrificed his lifelong dream, and was already in forward motion, knowing she could still accept or reject him. A few tears spilled over her eyelashes as she leaned forward and kissed him very softly. "I have never wanted anything more."

Giving a shout of jubilation, he slid the ring on her finger, drew her into his arms, and kissed her again. "I've missed you," he whispered, and she rested her forehead on his shoulder.

"I've missed you, too."

"Jessica, I need you to promise me something." His voice was serious again, and she drew back slightly to see his face.

"What's that?"

"I need you to promise me that from this day forward, no matter how hard things get, no matter how scared you are, you won't leave. And I'll promise you the same. I don't want to take our marriage lightly. I don't want to think of it as something we can 'do' when it's fun and pleasant and throw in the towel on when it gets hard. Jess, I will do everything in my power to be the best husband to you and the best father to the girls that I can possibly be. I will always do what I can to make life wonderful. I will pour my everything into our marriage. And I promise I will never so much as look at another woman in any sort of a lustful, wishful or comparative way. I promise you that.

"But I need to know that when things get tough, which I'm sure they will at times, because relationships are always a challenge, that you will stay and work it out with me," he continued. "I need to know that we will stay where we are and talk about it until we figure it out. I don't want to live in fear that the moment something isn't perfect, you're going to leave again. If you need time to process, fine, you can have it. If you need to process internally before we talk things out, then okay, process all you want. But promise me you won't leave, and you won't call it quits on us again."

Fully understanding the weight and sincerity of what she was promising, Jessica nodded. "I promise. I realized some things the last few weeks, too, and one of them is that I don't ever want to live life without you, Joe Colby. Even if it's hard, even if it's not always fun, even if circumstances are stressful and everything is going wrong, I want to get through it *with* you. I want to live life by your side," Jessi paused and took a deep breath. "You are not my father and I am not my mother. With God's help, we're going to make it to our first anniversary and our tenth and our thirtieth and our fiftieth and as many more years as the LORD gives us."

Joe's grin was instant and bright, warming her heart like nothing else could. "You're absolutely right. We are." He leaned forward and gave her another slow, sweet kiss.

"Joe, I've missed you the past few weeks. Like really, truly missed you with everything that is within me. I loved living life with you when we were just kids in high school, and I love living life with you now…even if it's just through text messages and phone calls. I love hearing your thoughts and your perspective. I love bouncing ideas off of you and having conversations. I love being with you. I love that you are confident and peaceful, full of joy and always making me laugh. You're handsome and after all these years, I feel drawn to you in a way I've never been drawn to another human being." Jessi reached out to weave her fingers between his, her eyes shining as they moved back to his ruggedly handsome face.

"I love watching you with our girls. I love how you make them giggle, how you make them feel safe, how you make them feel loved and secure, how you make me feel all of those things, too… I love who you are and what you're about. I love that you know what you believe, and you put everything you have into following God's will for your life. I love how loyal and devoted you are...how you've waited for me, how you've honored and loved me, even when I never would have known. I love that you are honest, full of integrity and so worthy of respect."

"When I got on that airplane six years ago and left you, I wondered," Jessi paused and licked her lips, taking a moment to steady her voice and blink the tears out of her eyes. "I wondered if I had just made the biggest mistake of my life. I couldn't picture life without you, but I was so afraid that if I stayed, I wouldn't be enough. I thought I would hold you back, and you would become dissatisfied....that I would be a disappointment in your life." She held up a hand to silence his argument. "And almost four weeks ago, when I got on that airplane and flew home without you...without my ring...without a promise to spend my life with you...I wondered again if I had made the biggest mistake of my life. But, Joe, I was so afraid that what we have, this love that we've always shared, I was afraid that it would grow cold. I convinced myself that I would rather live my life without you, always wishing I could have you, than to have you and lose you. But Joseph Colby, after trying to go back and rethink, re-plan, and re-accept a life without you, I realized that what I am more afraid of than being a disappointment, not being enough, or losing you, is never having you. I realized that giving up on you and on us *would* be the biggest mistake of my life...a mistake that I can't afford to make...a mistake that I refuse to make.

"So, Joe, this is me being super real and honest and laying aside all my attempts at protecting myself and my heart. This is me taking down every wall I have ever put up and saying that I love you, and I want to be your wife. I want to raise our girls with you, grow old with you, and go through life with you."

Joe leaned in for a kiss, his green eyes shining. "Marry me tonight?" She laughed, the sound raw with emotion, and wrapped her arms around his neck, leaning her forehead against his shoulder. She took a few moments to compose herself, her heart feeling exposed and vulnerable. Joe smoothed her hair back from her face. A slow sigh escaped from between her lips as his sweet affection assured her that she was safe with him. He pressed a kiss against her temple.

"I'm just kidding. I want the beautiful wedding we've envisioned. I want to see you in your white dress, and I want to marry you standing on the sand with my mom and dad watching and with Kara beside you and with your mom and dad and Jari as witnesses. I want to commit my heart, my body and my life to you with our daughters next to us. I want to take you as my wife before God and our family in a beautiful ceremony that we will always have to remember and treasure," he told her.

Joe's soft words soaked into Jessica, and she didn't say anything for several long moments as she tried to memorize his words, the tone of his voice, the thickness of emotion and the way it felt for him to hold her as he painted such a beautiful picture. She felt the longing for their wedding day grow steadily until it filled her. She knew he was experiencing the same thing when he pressed a kiss to the side of her face, then pulled back saying, "Hurry, let's find a house. May can't come soon enough!"

Letting go of the sweet, tender moment, Jessica laughed softly, agreeing, and stood up to get them each another slice of pizza. Joe found the housing section of the newspaper and pulled it free from the rest, taking them back to a safe place.

They spent the rest of the evening making a budget to see what they could afford, and then looking for apartments or houses that fit their budget and their needs with a good location close to where Joe would practice with the team all summer. They paused at eight o'clock to call the girls and tell them goodnight together. After Joe talked to each of their daughters for several minutes, they resumed their search. When they had made it through all of the listings and circled several to look at the next day, they watched a movie and called it a night, with Joe promising to meet her outside in the hall at eight the next morning.

Seventeen

The entire situation seemed absolutely preposterous considering that twenty-four hours earlier, there had been no wedding in her future, no fiancé, no plan of moving – nothing; nothing but her job in D.C., the girls, and the reality that she had once again chosen a life of being alone – a life void of Joe Colby. Yet here they were, pulling into an apartment complex, looking for somewhere to move to after they returned from their wedding in St. Lucia.

"Well, it seems like a nice complex," Joe commented, pulling her out of her thoughts as he drove by the stone sign that wore the name 'The Heights'. The entrance was landscaped nicely with a small waterfall and a pond, with promises of being a thing of beauty come spring. Jessi pulled her fitted wool coat slightly tighter. Regardless of whether or not she would soon live in Minnesota, she didn't think she would ever learn to love the long winters.

"The girls would like the pool," she observed, looking at the large, Caribbean-styled area that housed a large swimming pool, two water slides, a hot tub, dozens of lounge chairs and several grass umbrellas.

Joe shot her a sideways grin. "I think I'd enjoy the hot tub…we should make that an evening tradition." Jessi felt herself blush as she looked away.

"There's a nice playground, adequate parking…" she continued.

"What's the building number?" Joe asked, coming to a fork in the road, studying the sign that gave directions to different apartment buildings.

"Twenty-three," she answered, glancing through the classifieds until she found the right ad and the details she had written beside it after talking to the owner. "Unit thirty-four." Joe nodded, turning left. "There it is," Jessi told him seconds later, and he pulled into a parking place.

"You ready?" he asked, winking at her as he opened her door. Her smile was bright.

"Ready to take the first step toward making a life together? Ready for making concrete decisions about what life will look like for us after we get married? Ready to share a home and a family with you?" Jessi leaned forward and kissed Joe softly. "Absolutely."

His grin was cheerful and boyish as he grabbed her hand and led her up the sidewalk. "That's what I like to hear. Come on! I'm ready to find a house and for it to be May!" Jessica laughed and followed him up the outdoor stairway to the third floor. When he knocked on the door with the number thirty-four on the wall beside it, it swung open and warmth rushed out, making Jessi shiver just a little.

"Good morning! Come on in," an older gentleman said, holding the door open wide, inviting them to enter. As soon as they stepped inside, Jessica fell in love. The ceilings were tall, and a circular staircase was immediately to their right. "I'm Richard. I own this condo."

"I'm Joe." He stuck out his hand. "And this is my fiancé, Jessica." They all shook hands. Joe looked around and let out a slow whistle. "We were under the impression this was an apartment."

"Well, not exactly. It's kind of an odd deal. Let me tell you about it. This complex houses condominiums, apartment complexes, duplexes and even a few single-family homes. I've owned this condo since it was brand new… about two and a half years now. It's three bedroom, three and a half bath, and as you can see, two story. Two bedrooms are upstairs, each with their own bathroom. Down here, there's the living room, and that's a wood fireplace you see, the kitchen, dining room, guest bedroom and bathroom, and a powder room. The place is simple enough, but the complex part is that I'm really just renting it for the summer. Every year my daughter and three of her girl-friends live here while taking classes at the University. During the summer, they all go home or their separate ways, so it sits unoccupied. This year, I decided to try renting it out during the summer rather than letting it sit empty. So, with that being said, it's not available until the first week of May and needs to be empty by the third weekend in August. It's not long, and I know most folks aren't going to be interested in something like that, but I thought, hey, I might as well give it a try." His spiel complete, Richard stuffed his hands in his pockets and waited.

Joe looked at Jessica, then back at Richard. "We could possibly still be interested. We'd have to talk about it. We were expecting to have to sign a six or twelve month lease." Richard nodded. "However...well, we could possibly still be interested. Do you mind if we take a look around?"

"Feel free," Richard answered, motioning for them to go ahead. Jessica followed Joe up the steps and into the first bedroom. It wasn't huge, but it was decent, and it had its own bathroom. The walls were a pale yellow, and Jessica smiled as she pictured the girls' white and lavender décor in the sunshiny room.

Alone and out of ear shot, Joe turned to her. "You know, that could actually be perfect."

"I know. I was thinking the same thing."

"It's a little weird, and I wonder if we would feel rushed, but hopefully I will know if I have a spot on the team by then. By August maybe we can make more perma-nent plans – whether that's moving somewhere else, or find-ing a house and settling down here in the Twin Cities."

Jessica nodded slowly. "This room would work for the girls."

Joe nodded. "And it's nice that it's on the same floor as the master bedroom."

"Yeah, I like that," she agreed. After checking out the walk-in closet, she followed Joe into the next bedroom, which turned out to be a sprawling master suite. The jetted tub and large, walk-in tile shower made the bathroom, while a painted soffit and built-in window seat added style and flare to the oversized bedroom.

"Your bedroom furniture would look great in here," Joe told her, and she nodded in agreement. "Would this be big enough for your clothes?" he asked in mock seriousness, motioning to the large closet. She hit his arm, and he laughed. He pulled her into his arms and planted a quick kiss on her lips before simply holding her close, letting his eyes drift around the room. "Think, Jess. We could share this room. You and me." He didn't say anything else, nor did he need to. She cuddled in against him, wrapping her arms around his solid waste and giving him a hug.

After several moments, they moved on, going back downstairs and checking out the living room and kitchen before looking in the small guest bedroom and bathroom. The kitchen was sleek and stylish, the appliances nearly new. The style of the entire space was trendy and Jessica liked it. Regardless of how short their time in the condo would be, her furniture would look good in it, it was a space she could feel comfortable in, and she would feel good about inviting guests over. Finishing their tour and coming back into the living room, they found Richard sitting on the sofa, warming his hands in front of a roaring fire he had just lit. "What do you think?" he asked, glancing up.

Joe's grin was quick and encouraging. "You've got yourself a great condo here. We really like it."

Richard flashed his own grin, his chest puffing out just a little. "Thanks. I think it was a great find, too."

Checking his watch, Joe continued. "Well, Richard, we have several more apartments to look at today, but we sure appreciate you taking the time to show us your place. We'll definitely keep it in mind."

"I hope you don't mind me asking, but are you looking to make some decisions pretty quick, or will it still be awhile? I have another couple who wants to come look at it this evening, and another showing set-up for tomorrow. You were the first ones to look at it, though, and you seem like nice kids, so if you want it, I'd love to save it for you."

"That's good to know," Joe told him with a modest dip of his head. "We'll be making a decision by the end of the weekend, but if we're leaning toward this one, we'll let you know just as soon as possible."

"That sounds good. Good luck to you guys. I wish you the best," Richard told them, standing to shake Joe's hand again. After a quick goodbye, Joe took Jessi's hand as they went back out into the cold, down the stairs and to the car. She plugged the address of the next apartment into the GPS, while Joe shut her door and went around the car to get in.

Once inside, as he put the car in reverse, he glanced at her. "Was that it?" It warmed her heart how well he knew her.

"Probably. But I want to look at these others, just to be sure."

"I thought you'd say that." He was grinning again. "That's why I told him what I did. I suspect we'll be calling him back yet tonight, though, don't you?"

"What do you think about the timeframe? Do you think we'll like that in the end or wish we could stay longer?" Joe thought about her question for several seconds before answering.

"I'm not sure, but I think we'll have more direction by then and can make wiser decisions about our long-term plans at that point." Jessi nodded thoughtfully, agreeing.

The next apartment was twenty minutes away and closer to the stadium. Rent jumped a hundred dollars a month due to location, but they thought the forty minutes off his round-trip commute time might be worth it. The apartment was also in a nice complex, but was one-story and only a two bedroom. Still, the floor plan was spacious and comfortable.

"We could do without a guest room," Jessica observed once they climbed back into their car. Joe nodded. "And I really liked the kitchen and the view from the living room. The girls and I could look out the window and see where you are. They would like that." Again Joe nodded. "What are your thoughts?"

Joe took several moments before answering. "A year is a long time to be in a lease considering our current lack of definite direction. Come the end of summer, we'll be in a better place to sign a lease like that, but I'm not sure if we can commit to twelve months just yet. I mean, Jess, in a year we could have another baby...or two if we had twins again. Think about four kids in a two bedroom apartment."

"I highly doubt we would have twins twice."

Joe waved away her reasoning. "Still, a lot can happen in a year."

This time Jessica nodded. "That's true. The shorter commute would be nice, though. It would mean you being home more."

"That does sound nice," Joe conceded. "Okay, let's keep it in mind. Where's the next one?" Jessica plugged the next address into the GPS, and they were off again. They looked at two more, neither of which they liked, then stopped for a quick lunch. After lunch they looked at four more, three of which they crossed off, and one that went into the 'maybe' category. At dinner that evening, they talked through the advantages and disadvantages of each place, and came to the conclusion that they both felt the most peaceful about the first condo. Not only did they like the location, the complex, and the floor plan, but the short lease made it the most logical choice.

"Do you feel good about that decision?" Joe asked, searching Jessica's face.

She nodded, smiling. "I feel great about that decision."

"I do too," he told her. "I feel really peaceful about it."

Her eyes were shining again. "Make the call!" Joe did, excusing himself from the table so as not to be rude to those around them. When he came back, his grin stretched from one side of his face to the other.

"Do we have a house?" Jessi asked expectantly, her own face lighting up. He slid into the booth next to her and planted a kiss on her lips.

"We sure do! There we go, Jess! It's the first tangible step toward our life together. After we get married, we have a house to live in. Praise the LORD!"

"At least for three months," she added, and he laughed.

"At least for three months," he agreed.

~~~~~

"So, are you nervous about this week?" Jessica asked, straightening Joe's collar. They were standing in the airport just outside the security checkpoint, where they would go their separate ways in just a few minutes. He would go to the gym to work out before going back to the hotel to get some sleep before showing up at training camp the next morning. She would get on a plane and fly back to D.C., where she would pick up the girls, go home, do laundry and get some sleep before going to work.

"Nervous about getting pounded? Yes! These guys have been consistently working out, playing the game, getting ready, and I…have been going to class and eating cheeseburgers."

Jessi grinned, glancing over his long-sleeved t-shirt, noting how the fabric drew tight over his arms, shoulders and chest. He may not have played much football in the past couple of years, but he had certainly stayed in shape. "I don't see cheeseburgers." His expression turned shy, and he grinned even as he shrugged modestly. "You're going to do great," she finished.

"Well, I'd say we had a pretty productive weekend,"
~~~~~

he commented, changing the subject. She hid a smile and went with it.

"Yes, I'd say we did."

"We made up, called the wedding back on, made a budget, found a house…"

"Started looking for a church, went swimming, and got you in a couple of good workouts," Jessica finished, smiling up at him. He grinned, and his expression softened. He reached out and touched her face.

"Thanks for coming, Jess."

"I wouldn't have missed this." Silence stretched between them for several seconds as they studied one another, sadness seeping in as the impending goodbye loomed. Joe reached out and hooked a piece of hair behind her ear.

"You know, I've learned to really hate going to airports with you. It's a place I'd rather just stay clear of."

Jessica grinned and bit her lip, then took a step closer. "Maybe this will help redeem them." She reached up and kissed him slowly, linking her hands behind his neck. When the kiss ended, he followed it up with another, then took a deep breath, a smile on his face.

"Promise me that the next time I see you, we'll be getting married."

"I promise. In less than four weeks, Joe Colby, I'll see you at the airport in St. Lucia and in four weeks and five days, I'll meet you out on the beach. I'll be in my wedding dress, and you'll be in your suit, and we will commit to spend the rest of our lives together as husband and wife."

"I wish it were tomorrow instead of four weeks from now," he told her, pouting. She laughed and hugged him tight.

"Me too."

"What if I just kidnap you and keep you here until it's time to fly to St. Lucia?" he asked, wrapping her tightly in his strong arms so she couldn't move. She didn't mind at all.

"It's tempting," she agreed.

"Very."

Finally, after another kiss, he released her and stepped back. After a final farewell, she entered the line to go through security, then made her way through the airport, letting the realization sink in that this would soon be her home airport. After they returned from their honeymoon, as long as Joe landed a spot on the team – which she was sure he would – this would be the airport they flew into and out of, the airport they would pick family up from when they came to visit and the airport they would fly out of as a family when they went home for the holidays. The reality of the life they were about to start in Minnesota began to sink in as she walked through the terminal, looking for her gate.

While waiting for her flight to board, she called Kara, Jari, and her mom, reporting on the events of the weekend, answering questions, laughing and crying with each of them and celebrating the fact that the wedding was back on. Right before she boarded, she called Joe to talk for just a few more minutes while they were both still in the same state. Hearing her call to board, she hung up and got on the airplane to make the trip home, leaving Joe for the last time. From her seat on the plane, she sent him a text message, sharing the thought that consumed her mind. 'I can't wait to spend the rest of my life with you.'

Eighteen

"Mommy, do I look pretty?" Jessica turned from where she was talking to Joe on her cell phone, and a smile filled her face as she caught sight of Kamryn. They had set aside the afternoon to find something for the girls to wear to the wedding and were just getting started. Tears threatened to spill from her eyes, but she blinked them back.

"Joe, I've got to go. Kamryn has her first dress on," Jessi explained, hanging up as she crossed the distance separating her from her sweet daughter.

The little girl who, just a few short months ago was lying in a hospital bed fighting for her life, was standing in front of her in a pale peach cotton dress that was sleeveless, modest and tea-length. Her casts were gone, and she was beautiful and petite, her green eyes and soft, wispy blonde hair set off by the peach-colored dress. Jessica knelt in front of her and took her by her little shoulders.

"Kamryn, you look absolutely beautiful! Absolutely beautiful," she repeated again before kissing the sweet girl's forehead. Kamryn beamed, taking up her skirt and twirling back and forth just a little.

Kelsi burst out of the dressing room in an identical dress, Jari right behind her, and threw her hands up in the air, "Ta-da! What do you think, Mommy?" Jessi laughed, gathering the little brunette up in her arms and kissing her, too.

"You look stunning, Kels! Absolutely stunning!" Both girls were all smiles, satisfied with their mom's praise. "What do you girls think? Do you like these dresses?" Kelsi studied Kamryn's dress and Kamryn studied Kelsi's, then they turned to the full-length mirrors and looked at their own. Finally, Kelsi gave a decisive nod of her head.

"I like them. This is the dress I want," she told Jessi and Jari, turning to face them. Kamryn turned, too, following her sister's lead.

"Me too. I like it because it matches Aunt Kara's."

"It's true, they do match Kara's almost perfectly. I love them, girls! Absolutely love them! You are going to look like little island flowers standing out on the beach in those dresses! Just look at yourselves – you're beautiful!" Jari gushed, snapping pictures. The little girls giggled.

"I like them too! Alright, that was easy. Now, let's find some shoes to go with those pretty dresses," Jessi told her daughters, motioning a sales clerk over. The girls tried on several pairs of shoes, but they were all too fancy or too casual.

"Mommy, I was wondering…well, I was thinking…" Kamryn stopped, turning her eyes from Jessica to the ground. Jessi stopped what she was doing and looked up from the boxes of shoes sitting around her to the quieter of her twin girls.

"What, Baby? What were you thinking?"

"Well, aren't you and Daddy getting married on the beach…like a sandy beach?"

"Yes."

"Well, are there stickers in the sand?"

Jessica shook her head. "I wouldn't think so."

"Well, I was wondering if we could maybe not wear any shoes with our dresses…since we can't find any. I was thinking it might be nice to feel the sand between our toes and not have to worry about getting sand in our shoes."

Jessica weighed the idea, then glanced at Jari, who was smiling. Jessi turned her attention back to Kamryn, her face blossoming into a bright smile. "I think that is a great idea!"

"You do?" Kamryn asked, beaming.

"Absolutely! It will fit with the casual feel of the wedding, it will be more comfortable for you girls, and I love it. What do you think, Kels?"

Kelsi spent a few more moments looking longingly at the glass slipper-style shoes she was wearing that had long since been out of the running, and finally nodded. "I think that's a good idea, Kammy. That way if everyone talks too long, we can wiggle our toes in the sand." Her last comment drew laughter from Jari and Jessi.

"Well, that settles it!" Jari told them, hoisting Kelsi up to her hip. "We'll take these two peach dresses and none of the shoes," she told the clerk who had been helping them. Kamryn clapped her hands, excited that they had chosen her idea.

Jessica helped the girls take off their new dresses and handed them over the dressing room door to Jari. She helped them into their denim capris and brightly colored polos. Jessica re-did Kammy's hair while Kelsi slipped on her pink flip flops and then Jessica straightened Kelsi's ponytail while Kammy put her purple shoes on. Once both girls were completely dressed, Jessi pulled them both into a tight hug.

"I love you girls," she told them, holding them for just a moment. "Do you know that?"

They both giggled. "We know, Mommy!" they answered in unison. Jessica smiled and released them.

"Good! Let's go get some ice cream!"

"Yay!" The girls exploded into happy dancing, squeals and clapping. Still smiling, Jessica reached over them to open the dressing room door, and then followed them up to the front of the store where Jari was just finishing up.

Once everyone was buckled, Jessi turned the car toward the girls' favorite ice cream shop. They were busy in the backseat discussing what kind of ice cream they would order.

"Three weeks, Jess. Are you ready?" Jessica glanced at her step-mom and thought about everything that had happened over the past seven years, the past year, the past six months.

"I wish it were tomorrow," she answered confidently.

Jari's expression was tender and pleased. "How's the packing going?"

Jessica made a face. "Another reason I wish the big day were already here."

Jari laughed and reached over to squeeze Jessi's hand. "You'll get there. I can come help this weekend if you'd like."

Jessi nodded. "That would be wonderful. I'm not exactly sure what I was thinking when I told Melinda I could work up through five p.m. the day before we leave."

"I wondered the same thing," Jari admitted. After a pause, she continued. "How do you feel about leaving your work?"

"Weird," Jessi admitted. "It's become such a part of my life. I can't imagine hearing about something on the news and not going...not being there to help people...not being there to help them sift through the remnants of their lives."

"You've wanted this for a long time, cared about a lot of people, felt a lot of hurt, studied for so many years. It must feel strange leaving it all behind."

Jessi nodded. "It does. But I have a feeling I'll get involved in one way or another once we get to Minnesota. I can't imagine not being involved. Whether through volunteering or getting a part-time job that wouldn't require travel, I know I'll get back in the field. I might move to Minnesota where everything is new, but one thing that will be the same is the multitude of hurting people who I'm sure will be around me."

"Hurting people who need Jesus," Jari murmured.

"Hurting people who need Jesus," Jessi echoed.

Cheers went up in the backseat as Jessica turned the SUV into the parking lot of the ice cream shop. "I'm getting cheesecake ice cream with raspberries and graham cracker crust. What are you getting?" Jari asked, turning in her seat toward the girls in the back.

"Rainbow chip ice cream with Skittles and gummy worms and strawberries!" Kelsi announced jubilantly.

"Sounds sweet and wormy," Jari responded, drawing a laugh from the girls. "Kam?"

"Chocolate!"

"Anything in it?" Jari pressed.

"Nope, just chocolate."

Jari elbowed Jessica. "Like mother like daughter."

Jessi laughed. "That's my girl."

Nineteen

Jessi sat perfectly still, looking at the framed photo in her hands. It was a picture of her and the girls playing in the leaves. It had been taken in the park by the mall she and Jari shopped at, a park she had gone to often as a child with her own mother, while she was pregnant, and since the girls were born. She had a lot of memories in that park...and now it was a park she likely wouldn't visit again.

She wrapped the frame in two sheets of newspaper and put it in the box in front of her. She reached for the next framed photo – Kelsi's four-year-old picture that was taken last summer. The spunky little girl looked as sweet as could be, her little face propped up on her fists, lying on her belly on the old stone park bench, her bare feet crossed and up in the air. Jessica reached up for Kamryn's also, to look at them together. Kamryn was perched on the edge of the bench, a parasol shading her from the sun, intent on something crawling on the ground. She wasn't even looking at the camera, but her profile had been so precious, Jessica had decided to frame the photo anyway.

She would have to find a new photographer to take the girls' pictures and their yearly family photo once they got to Minnesota. It was another thing to add to her to-do list, another thing that would be changing after the move. Taking a deep breath, she wrapped the photos and put them into the box as well. Standing, she moved her box to the entertainment center and continued taking down photos.

There were pictures from the day the girls were born. With one tiny, red infant in each arm, Jessica looked exhausted, but indescribably happy. The emotions of the day welled up in her again, and she felt the same pride and joy she had felt as she held her girls for the very first time. There were pictures of them as smiling, cooing babies, as toddlers learning to walk, of birthday parties, Christmases and fun times with family. Her dad and Jari were in several.

Jari – a woman who had given her everything and made the sky the limit for her over the past six years. An enemy who had become more than just an ally – she had become Jessica's best friend. Sadness surged as she realized there would be no more Saturday shopping trips, family game nights, or mid-week lunches. Jessi was careful not to let the tears fall as she very carefully wrapped the framed photos and added them to the box.

Next, she picked up a picture of her, Carla, Maybelle, Kelsi and Kamryn. They had visited the Library of Congress and were standing on the front stairs in the picture. Jessi bit her lip, holding back a sob, realizing that she would no longer be ten minutes away from her grandmother or a short car ride away from her mom. Those two women had been a part of her life since before she could remember, and living life without them would undoubtedly feel as if a part of herself was missing. She had never realized how much she loved and enjoyed her mom until she'd been forced to move back to D.C., and leave Carla behind. Now, her heart ached as she thought of the reality of being so far away from her once again. She closed her eyes and took long breaths as she wrapped and placed the picture.

When she lifted the next picture, her tears were forgotten and her heart surged. She studied the picture that she had placed there only weeks before, after returning from Minnesota. It was from last Christmas. Joe was on the couch at his parents' house in Glendale. Kamryn, in all her casts, was on his lap with a Santa hat on her head, and Kelsi was up on her knees on the couch beside him, her arm around his neck. Jessi was bending over the back of the couch, her face right beside Joe's, and he, at the last moment, had turned his head and kissed her cheek. She was laughing.

Impulsively, she leaned forward and kissed the picture. Packing her apartment, leaving everything and everyone behind was hard and sad, but he – the man in the picture in front of her – was worth it all.

~~~~~

"Joe! Buddy! Was that your last final? Are you done?"

Joe looked up and saw his friend Matt coming toward him. He bobbed his head. "Just finished my last one."

"Doesn't it feel good? I just finished, too. Now, three months of lazy summer days before hitting the books again next fall. I'm telling you, I'm looking forward to that! What are you doing with your summer?"

Joe quickly realized the obvious. "Matt, I must have forgotten to tell you...I'm not coming back next fall." He noted the shocked expression that filled his friend's face. "I'm moving to Minnesota to play football. ...And I'm getting married next week."

"Wow. No, you hadn't told me. Pretty sure I would have remembered that..." Joe grinned. "That's a lot of change."

"It is a lot of change," Joe agreed, "but it's the right thing to do...it's what I want."

"Huh. Well, are you excited?"

Joe shook his head, grinning. "More than I can even express. What are you doing this summer?"

"Going home for the first half, then to Venezuela on a mission trip for the last. I'll get back to the States just three days before classes start."

"Awesome. Have you been out of the country before?"

"Never."

"It's going to change your life," Joe told him. "I went to southern Mexico a couple of years back and...you really aren't the same person by the time you get home."

"That's what I've heard. I'm pretty excited about it. I'm ready for the experience, ready to meet the people."

"You're going to do great," Joe told him before checking his watch. "Hey, I gotta go. I fly out to get married to-morrow, and I still have to finish up at my apartment. But I'm really glad I ran into you. You take care this summer."

"Yeah, you too, Joe. I'll be watching for you on TV next year," Matt told him with a grin, then walked backward a couple of steps before turning and continuing on his way.

Joe walked to where his car was parked, the odd realization settling over him that this was his last time on campus. He had spent the last two years studying, learning, and encountering God here, yet when he got into his car and drove away, he might never see it again. Unlike his classmates, who were returning in the fall, he would be moving to Minnesota and starting a new life.

Despite his rush, he turned at the end of the sidewalk and looked back. His eyes moved over the brick buildings, the lush green landscaping that announced spring had finally come to Michigan, and the large open yards. His eyes fell on benches where he had sat to engage in dozens of conversations with faculty and students. He glanced at the library where he had spent countless hours studying. He looked to the church where he had attended hundreds of services throughout the week and on Sunday mornings. Almost seeing the page turning and the chapter closing in his mind, he turned and continued through the parking lot to his car.

A chapter might be closing, but a new one was opening. He had no regrets, and was certainly not having second-thoughts. He pictured the girl who would meet him in St. Lucia – the blue-eyed, dark haired, intriguing, mystifying, and at so many times, frustrating beauty he was leaving all of this behind for. He thought of the pale-eyed little girls who would likely stick to him like glue for the next several days and months. He thought of the new door that was opening in front of him – the possibility of playing professional football. No, he didn't have any regrets. Not one. It was different, that was for sure, but he couldn't be more excited.

To finally have Jessica Cordel as his wife, to be installed as the permanent, present leader of his little family, to play a game he loved, was all exciting. There was no room for anything but excitement – excitement and relief – relief that the wait was finally over, that everything would soon be as it should, and that the heartbreak of the last six years was finally over.

At least he hoped it was over. His mouth curved up into something between a grimace and a grin. He was hoping Jessi didn't try to back out one more time. If she did, there would be no more respecting her decisions. He would find her, catch her up in his arms and carry her to the altar. That thought made him grin. He loved her through and through, and he knew that she loved him, too. There was no way he wasn't going to marry her in a week.

Once he got back to his apartment, he climbed the stairs, unlocked his front door and went in. All of his furniture was gone. He had sold it the weekend before. Nothing he had was nice enough to keep. He had bought it all at garage sales when he moved into his apartment, and he had sold it the same way. The belongings he was taking consisted of the books he had collected, his clothes, a few framed photographs and his worn black Bible.

With his last class completed, he slid the textbook and Bible from his backpack. He put the textbook in the box of books and his Bible in his suitcase. Then, he folded the flaps of the box down and taped it.

When he was finished, he drove to the post office where he stood in line and then paid to ship his boxed belongings to their new apartment in Minnesota. He needed to call Jessi and let her know that everything was done. Excitement was steadily building within him. Checking his watch as he left the post office, he realized the moving truck should be leaving Jessi's house in a few minutes. He decided to wait until later to call, knowing she would be busy wrapping things up.

He went to the gym to get in a workout, and called her on his way home. After hanging up, he took a shower and laid down on the floor in his room to catch a few hours of sleep. The floor was hard and uncomfortable, but his excitement for his impending vacation was more to blame for his insomnia than his sleeping conditions.

When he woke up five hours later to the obnoxious beeping of his alarm clock, he jumped up, brushed his teeth, fixed his hair, changed his clothes and packed his toiletries away in his suitcase. After one more walk-through of the apartment, he was satisfied he had everything. He zipped his suitcase shut, set it on its wheels and pulled it through the empty rooms. At the front door, he paused and turned to glance around the small apartment one last time.

The realization settled over him that he was leaving his childhood. He was leaving school, leaving his high school and college days, leaving the carefree life of a bachelor. In many ways, his youth was over. When he returned to America from St. Lucia, he would be returning to play pro football – no more college football. If he could land a spot on the team, it would be the real deal. He would also be returning with a wife and children – children that were his but hadn't necessarily felt like it for the past five years. He would be expected to provide and protect, lead and lay foundations.

His cell phone began ringing in his pocket, and as he pulled it out and saw Jessica's face filling the screen, he couldn't hold back a grin that felt like it stretched out his cheeks. He pulled the door shut and locked it as he answered. He was suddenly in a hurry to leave his apartment, leave his college town, leave his youth and his singlehood. The woman and two girls that would be waiting for him in St. Lucia were more than worth it all, and he couldn't wait to get to them.

Twenty

"Mommy, do you think Daddy will be waiting for us when we get to St. Lucia?" Jessica glanced at her watch. Joe's flight had been scheduled to get in half an hour after theirs, but they had been delayed at the airport in D.C., and were now running an hour and a half late.

"As long as his flight wasn't delayed, too, he should be," she answered, soaking in the delight and excitement she saw in her daughter's face.

"Kels, did you hear that? Daddy's going to be waiting for us in St. Lucia!" Kamryn called, leaning out to see around Jessica to her sister across the aisle.

"Probably," Jessi reminded. Kelsi clapped her hands, doing a little dance in her seat and Jari and Bill, sitting beside her, laughed.

"Kammy, what are you most looking forward to this week?" Maybelle asked, turning away from the airplane window to fall into conversation with her great-granddaughter.

"Getting a daddy!" was Kamryn's easy reply.

"There will be lots of things to do. There are beaches to play on, sandcastles to make, and all of your grandmas, grandpas, aunts, uncles and cousins will be there to play with. There will be the ocean to swim in, your pretty dress to wear, and all of the exotic flowers to smell. Are you sure that's what you're most excited about?" Maybelle had a twinkle in her eyes.

"Yep! I'm sure," Kamryn told her simply. "Getting a daddy – a real daddy that lives with us and never leaves – *and* wearing my pretty new dress *and* building sandcastles. I do love building sandcastles."

Maybelle laughed. "So do I. Maybe we can build one together!"

From her spot on the other side of Kamryn, Jessica leaned her head back against the seat and smiled. The last few days had been a blur. There had been a lot of loose ends to tie up between quitting her job, getting everything into the moving truck and on its way, finalizing the details of the reservations and the ceremony, the final fitting on her dress and a dozen other things that stood between her and St. Lucia. But now, cruising thousands of feet above the ocean, she felt her nerves calming, her stress dissipating, and her excitement growing until she felt like dancing in her seat just as Kelsi had.

An hour later, as they touched down on the runway, her heart began pounding faster. She couldn't wait to see Joe – to throw her arms around him and hold on tight. After today, she would never have to let go of him again. Not in the way that made the days ahead look bleak, her responsibilities too large to carry, and her heart break. In just a few days they would be getting married and they would be joined for life.

Suddenly, she felt butterflies in her stomach – butterflies that came from the thought of seeing him, of being with him. She ran her hand down the front of her sundress, smoothing the yellow-printed fabric, hoping to smooth her nerves as well.

"Jess, why don't you run on in and see your fiancé? We'll get the girls and the luggage," her dad offered, leaning out around Jari.

"Oh, I can help," she argued, waving away his offer even though she desperately wanted to accept.

"Don't argue with your father," Carla said from behind her. That made Jessi laugh, realizing again how truly blessed she was by the reconciliation in her family. It might be an odd family torn by divorce and added to by a stepmom and a step-dad, but there was peace, forgiveness, respect and kindness. Jessica sent a prayer of thanks up to heaven, even as she unbuckled her seatbelt.

"Alright, if you guys insist!" she told them, grinning. She made her way through the aisle, slipping between people who were retrieving their luggage from the overhead compartments, and hurried up to the front of the plane. After stepping into the wide tunnel that led to the airport terminal, she broke out of the crowd and her steps quickened.

As she stepped into the terminal, she scanned the small crowd. There weren't many waiting, and her eyes landed quickly on a young man in jeans, a white t-shirt and a green baseball cap with sunglasses propped up on the bill of his cap. Her heart jumped, and the butterflies in her stomach turned to birds. A quick grin spread across Joe's face as his eyes met hers, and he jumped over a row of chairs separating them, jogging toward her. She ran the remaining distance between them and threw her arms around his neck, letting out a sigh of relief as his lips found hers.

"I thought you were never going to get here!" Joe told her as the kiss ended. He stood still, just holding her, her face nestled into his shoulder.

"Me too. It has really been a long time coming." She looked up in time to catch his grin.

"That it has. I've been waiting for this day for a long time, Jessica Cordel. The wedding can't get here soon enough." She kissed him again, slowly, sweetly, and when she broke off the kiss, he grinned down into her eyes before lifting her off the ground and twirling her around, making her laugh. As he set her feet lightly on the ground again, she caught sight of familiar faces.

"There they are!" she exclaimed, pulling Joe toward the others, waving.

"Daddy!" Kamryn and Kelsi spotted them at the same time and, wriggling to be set down, came running as soon as their feet touched the floor. Jessica couldn't stop smiling as she watched Joe squat down, his arms open wide in welcome. Kelsi got to him first, with her sister just a step behind her. Both girls flung themselves into Joe's waiting arms, hugging him around the neck. There was an eruption of giggles as he wrapped his arms around them and stood, their little flip-flop-clad feet dangling, jiggling them around this way and that as he hugged them.

Kamryn put her hands on either side of his face and looked seriously into his eyes. "Tell me one thing, Daddy."

Joe grinned. "Shoot."

"Have you built any sandcastles without me?" Jessica felt warmth spreading through her as Joe sent her an amused look over their daughter's head.

"No ma'am. I wouldn't dare. I wasn't even going to step foot out of this airport until I had you two and Mommy with me." Kelsi and Kamryn were all grins as the rest of the group approached. The girls were set on the ground so Joe could shake Bill and Tim's hands and hug the women. After just a few minutes of catching up, they found the arrivals screen to check on the status of the Colbys' flight. It was still on time, so they made their way through the airport as a group to set up camp at the gate their plane was just taxing up to.

While they waited for the Colby gang to make their way off the plane, Kelsi and Kamryn went to use the bathroom with Maybelle and Jari, Carla and Tim went after bottles of water, Bill made a phone call to the office to confirm things were going smoothly, and Joe pulled Jessi firmly against his side. She wrapped her arms around his waist and leaned her head against his chest, looking up at him, studying every feature, memorizing how he looked at that very moment. Looking down at her, he tugged on a piece of her hair, then bent down and kissed her very gently. "We are getting married in six days," he whispered softly.

Kara was first out of the tunnel. The blonde-haired, green-eyed woman looked as pixie-ish as she had as a teenager. Just seeing her made Jessi smile. Kara ran to where they stood waiting, throwing her arms around both of them at the same time. "You're getting married! You're getting married! You're getting married!" she sang, making them laugh as they embraced her. Justin was right behind her with a greeting and a handshake, his grin matching Joe's. Hannah and Chris were next, their smiles as big as their hugs. Kaitlynn twirled Jessica around, hugging her tight, as Jake pumped Joe's hand. Kimberly and Greg took a break from corralling the kids to embrace them both, their smiles bright, before following their little ones to where they had met up with Kelsi and Kamryn.

When the rush had passed, Hannah's eyes were shiny with unshed tears as she looped her arm through Jessi's. Joe took Jessica's other hand. The three of them started off together to meet Jari and the girls, who were now laughing and chattering away with the cousins.

"It's finally here. After all these years, after all the days that it seemed so impossible, it's finally here. Before you leave here, you'll have promised each other forever. Can you believe it?" Hannah asked, squeezing Jessi's arm.

Jessi let Joe answer as she allowed Hannah's words to settle. Hannah was right. What had started at a 7-Eleven in Glendale was finally about to end on a beach in St. Lucia. In the beginning she had felt so different – alone, angry, sad, confused. She had been so desperate to find someone who would love her, who could make her world make sense. For something that had started so badly, it sure was ending beautifully. "You've turned my mourning into dancing, You've made beauty from my ashes," she whispered, sending silent thanks up to heaven.

As Hannah left them to hug her granddaughters, Jessi snuggled back into Joe's side. She was thankful this ending was no ending at all, but rather a new beginning, a new chapter, a new life for her, Joe and their children. She had never been so excited, never wanted anything more in her entire life.

"I am so thankful for you, for this," she told him simply, looking up to meet his green eyes that were full of tenderness. "Before we leave here, I'll be your wife and you'll be my husband – for the rest of our lives." She felt the slow, happy smile spreading across her face.

~~~~~

The weather was perfect. It was almost sunset. A warm island breeze ruffled her dress. Palm trees lined her path. Her flowers were brilliant and tropical. She had looked at herself in the mirror long enough to know that her dress fit beautifully, her hair was perfect, her makeup exact. Her mom, Jari, Maybelle and Hannah had all ended their fussing fifteen minutes before and had gone out to take their seats. Kara walked in front of her, the girls following right behind their aunt. Flower petals fluttered down from their small fingers. Bill had his arm through hers. As they approached the beach, music floated softly to them on the warm air.

Her dad stopped, and she looked up at him in question. When he turned his eyes toward her, tears filled them. "Are you ready, Honey? Are you ready to get married?"

Jessi felt tears brim in her own eyes, and she swallowed hard as she smiled. "Yes, Daddy. I'm ready to get married."

"You make the most beautiful bride, and I only wish I had seized every moment of you being a little girl. As a father, I don't want to give you away today," Bill confessed. "But I know that you love that boy and that he loves you. He's a good man, and I have prayed for this day to come."

"You have?" she asked, hoping and praying she could remember this moment – this conversation that was proving to be the most tender, intimate moment she and her father had ever shared – for the rest of her life.

"I have." He framed her face with his hands. "Jessica, I am so proud of you." Jessi smiled, soaking in his words of affirmation – words she had longed to hear for a very long time. He let out a deep sigh as he looked up to see Kara and the girls walk out of the tree-lined walkway. "So, Baby Girl, it's time. Are you ready to become Joe Colby's bride?"

Biting her lip, Jessica smiled and nodded. "I'm ready, Daddy. So ready."

Leaning down, he kissed her cheek. And then, taking a deep, shuddering breath, he started them walking again. They stepped out of the trees, and the ocean spread out before them, dazzling under the last rays of the setting sun. The sky was a brilliant tapestry of breathtaking colors. The white beach stretched out for miles. The salt-tinged air smelled of flowers and ocean. The music changed. Their small party stood and turned. And as they rounded the last turn and stepped into the aisle, there he was.

Joe Colby was waiting for her at the altar. His chocolate hair was falling just right, his pale green eyes were electric, and as he had the very first time she met him, he was pulling her to him with some indescribable force that she felt at the very core of her being.

He was there. Waiting for her.

His expression was intense, for once he wasn't grinning. She could tell he was struggling against emotion, and she knew just how he felt. After everything they had been through together, after the journey they had been on, she was in her white dress and he was in his suit, waiting for her at the altar.

In just a few more steps, she would reach him. And then she was there, and he was coming forward to meet her. She left her father and went with him to stand before the pastor. And there, in front of the Caribbean Sea, with the sun setting behind them and their loved ones all around them, with their daughters standing beside them, they promised each other forever.

Epilogue

Joe carried the flaming cake through the kitchen and set it on the dining room table in front of his grinning daughters. Six candles lit the cake. Jessica started everyone singing, and the room full of family joined in.

Joe looked around at his parents, Justin and Kara, Kimberly and Greg and their children, Kaitlynn and Jake and their children, Bill and Jari, Tim and Carla, and Maybelle, and he smiled as he sang along with them. All of their family was here with them in Minnesota to celebrate the girls' special day.

As the song ended, Joe looked across the room and met Jessi's eyes. She smiled at him, and he noticed her hand lay protectively against her swollen belly as it did so often these days. He grew excited as he counted up the weeks until their third child, a boy, was due. Only seven more.

Kelsi and Kamryn blew out their candles, their eyes as big as their smiles, and Jessica bustled in to cut the cake. They had already enjoyed a feast for dinner, and the birthday cake was dessert. Next would come present opening, then a trip to the bowling alley, as requested by the girls. Joe was looking forward to the outing with all of the extended family.

As the chairs at the table were full, Joe took his cake and wandered into the living room. He found himself standing in front of the hearth as he often did, looking up at their wedding picture. Even after nine months of marriage, he was stunned by his wife's beauty, especially on the day of their wedding. She was truly a spectacular sight.

He felt warm hands start to knead at the stiff muscles in his shoulders. He leaned into Jessi's hands, still sore from his rigorous training schedule from the week.

After a lot of hard work, he had made Minnesota's football team. He certainly hadn't started his first season, but had ended up with more minutes of playing time than he ever expected, due to the starting quarterback taking it easy for several weeks, nursing an injury. Even after training intensively both individually and with his team, the pros had been much harder than he expected. College had barely begun to prepare him for the intensity level, both physically and mentally, of playing in the pros. Determined to be better prepared by the time preseason started, he was putting in extra workouts and practices, and was paying for it with sore muscles.

"That felt good," Joe told Jessica as she slipped her arm around his waist and came alongside him. She smiled up at him – that smile that always tugged on his heart.

"How's your cake?" she asked.

"Delicious," he told her, leaning down to plant a kiss on her lips. "You did a great job with it."

She leaned her head against his shoulder for just a moment, then took his hand and turned him back toward the kitchen. "We should have the girls open gifts so we can get to the bowling alley at a decent time."

"Good thinking," he answered, kissing her once more before they joined the others, wishing he could steal her away for several more minutes. He would have to see if his mom and dad would be interested in watching the girls some evening before they flew home, so he could take his wife out on a proper date. Stepping back into the kitchen and seeing that the girls were done with their cake, he grabbed both giggling six-year-olds, letting one dangle from each arm, and took them into the living room where their pile of gifts awaited them.

As he videotaped the present opening, he again thanked the LORD for his daughters' complete and total recovery from the nearly tragic car accident two Christmases before. One small scar on Kamryn's cheek was all that remained from the terrifying event.

He looked at both girls, beautiful, healthy, happy and whole, and he looked at his wife, who was glowing even as far along as she was in her pregnancy, and did something he did frequently throughout the days – he thanked the LORD for his family, for bringing them back together, and for bringing them all back to Him.

"You are the Alpha and Omega, the Beginning and the End. You don't stop in the middle. You finish what You start," he told the LORD under his breath. "It's been a long road, but this is worth it. Your ways are always better."

A NOTE FROM ANN

Dear Reader,

Despite Joe and Jessi's happy ending, finishing this book – and this series – was a sad day for me. Over the years, these characters have become such a part of my life, and the lives of my family. At my brother's football game not long ago, two twin girls sat down in front of us with their family. My mom turned to me and whispered, "Look! Its twin girls, just like Kelsi and Kamryn." Last fall as my husband and I were driving through D.C., he made the remark that should they be real, we should have called Joe and Jessi to see if they had time for dinner. Fictional characters or not, Joe, Jessi and the other characters in The Glendale Series have become friends, and saying goodbye to friends is never easy.

The two main themes of this book were very personal for me. Over and over in recent years, I have been left wondering if God changes His mind, and if He doesn't, why He sends us out in one direction, only to throw a curveball, and we suddenly find ourselves going in a completely new direction. Over and over, just when we think we know what we're doing and where we're going, something happens, and we realize we truly know nothing at all. After years of experiencing this phenomenon time after time after time, I don't even pretend to understand the ways of God, but this is what I know – His ways are always better. Sometimes, things happen that make it seem as if you've been absolutely wasting your time, energy and sometimes even your faith, but throughout the process of the journey, over and over He shows us that unexpected events that we immediately count as bad or unfortunate, are actually His mercy – His gifts – that clear the way and bring about His best in our lives. He has taught us the importance of being flexible and open to His moving. He has taught us to move with Him and embrace His journey for us rather than trying so desperately to cling to the path we think will get us to where we are one day meant to be, which in reality, only leads to an unfulfilling end, if not disaster.

Secondly, the reality of sacrifice that Joe had to face in the pages of this book has been something that has gripped my heart in the past few years. Each of us, as Christians, are told to pick up our cross and follow Jesus. While we're super familiar with that phrase and it sounds like a glorious, shiny task that is complete with Easter-morning-style mental pictures, the reality is that the cross is all about pain, humility and sacrifice; and we're commanded to join Him in His suffering. Each day, we are faced with opportunities to lay ourselves down for the sake of another, and more often than not, it's not convenient, comfortable or second-nature. At least not for me. Being unselfish and others-focused are not qualities that I was innately born with, yet, in His great love and sometimes humor, Jesus continues to give me almost constant opportunities to exercise both in laying down myself for the sake of another in my marriage, my family, my friendships and even new acquaintances. While it's not natural or overly enjoyable at times, over and over I sense the whisper of a promise that it is always worth it. Our willing participation in joining our Savior in laying down our lives, actually opens our hearts, our minds, our relationships and our circumstances to Him, inviting Him to come in and make the wrong things right. Additionally, through willingly choosing sacrifice, we are making room for Him to come in and take us to a new level in our relationship with Him.

In *Promising Forever*, when the story suddenly changes and Joe, with a new perspective, realizes that the broken engagement was just as much his fault as it was Jessi's, it honestly caught me by surprise, even as the writer. Selfishness and control creep up on us so quietly and slip in, so often uncaught under a pleasing layer of good intentions and being a good person. It reminded me to be on guard and to catch those little foxes that can spoil an entire vineyard (Song of Songs 2:15).

As hard as it was to see this series end and to say goodbye to Joe and Jessica, I'm thankful that my next series, Mothers of Glendale, will focus on familiar characters Jari, Carla and Hannah and that, in the midst of the stories of these three strong, resilient women, we'll check in on Joe and Jessi and their children from time to time. So, while this is the end of the series, it's not necessarily a final goodbye. If seeing this book and this series come to a close has made you sad, too, make sure you read the Mothers of Glendale series to stay connected.

As always, although I love to write, I write for my readers. With that constantly in mind, I would love to hear from you. I enjoy getting emails, hearing from you on facebook and getting to know you, so please, always feel free to drop me a note!

Until next time, may the One whose ways are always higher, show you the beauty of His intricate plans and give you peace and confidence that He always knows the way to the best!

Ann

A Special Preview of *One Desire,* Mothers of Glendale Book I

Life had changed. Again. Her heart felt heavy, her eyes stung. She walked through the quiet rooms of her house and felt their emptiness acutely. She paused at the refrigerator and looked at the drawings that covered it, then studied the photographs that lined the top. She smiled fondly at the precious faces smiling back at her. Closing her eyes, Jari Cordel let herself imagine her house full of precious little giggles and loud shrieks of laughter, as it had been just a month before. She imagined it full of life, full of love, full of friendship…and mostly, just full. Now, the large house just felt empty.

She moved her eyes to the most recent photograph on her fridge and a smile tugged the corners of her lips up. No matter how lonely she felt, Joe and Jessica's wedding day brought happy memories and the peace that comes from fulfilled promises. The picture was not one of the many professional photos from the wedding that Jari had hung just the week before, but was a candid snapshot that Joe's mother, Hannah, had shared.

After the wedding, with the setting sun behind them and the sand under their feet, Joe, in his suit, had dipped Jessi, wedding dress and all, over his knee and kissed her soundly. Their twin girls, Kelsi and Kamryn, were watching the moment transpire, both giggling. Impulsively, Jari ran her hand over the photograph, her heart swelling then sinking as it had so many times in the month since Joe and Jessi returned from their honeymoon to pick up the girls and move to their new home in Minnesota.

She turned swiftly, determined she would not cry again, but a sigh escaped before she could stop it. She began to wander the house again.

She had never before struggled with feelings of depression as she now was. Her life could be categorized in three distinct segments – childhood, her wild years and Jessi. As she sat down at the kitchen table, her mind raced back across the years, and she let her forehead rest against her arms.

Growing up in small town Kansas now felt as far away as an old dream, the kind you wake up from and can feel more than you can remember. Her life had seemed almost perfect – perfectly boring, perfectly predictable, and perfectly perfect in her eyes.

Her dad owned the tire shop in town. If you needed an oil change, new tires, new brakes or your tires balanced and rotated, you would undoubtedly end up at Skip's Tire Repair. Not only did he do the best work in town, he owned the only tire shop within forty miles.

As a young girl, she spent many afternoons and Saturdays at the shop. She learned to love the smell of old oil and new rubber – smells that still took her back to the small garage on second street, just eight blocks away from their home on Elm. Many afternoons she did her homework perched on a stack of new tires, watching her dad and his employees work as she tapped her forehead with her eraser in thought. She learned multiplication to the sudden ruckus of air compressors, which had ceased to startle her years earlier, the clatter of crow bars hitting the cement floor, and the high-pitched whine of an impact gun.

As she grew up, she was sent from her father's garage to her mother's flower shop. Instead of being surrounded by vehicles, tires, and loud noises, she was enveloped in the world of roses, gardenias, daisies, orchids and baby's breath every afternoon and on Saturdays from nine to five. With guidance from her mom, she was soon the fastest at wrapping a boutonniere and learned the delicate strategies of arranging a perfectly balanced bouquet of flowers. She helped her mother prepare the floral arrangements and decorate for countless weddings. She took orders and delivered bouquets for neighbors and fellow townspeople who were in love, in grieving or in trouble.

In a small town, a flower shop was more than just a business. Sure, there were bills to be paid, but at her mother's store, a funeral was not seen as an opportunity to make a profit. Tears went into every arrangement as she watched her mother grieve for the friend who had passed away. Wedding orders did not end the moment the last flower was delivered to the church. After the bouquets were finished, they changed into their dresses and attended the joyous event. Arrangements that were delivered to the hospital often resulted in a half-hour long chat with the patient and several phone calls once back at the shop to report on how they were doing. As she settled into her teen years, Jari began to think that a small town flower shop was exactly where she wanted to spend the rest of her life.

She played volleyball and cheered for the basketball team her sophomore year, made solid B's, and was fully planning to marry the boy who had been asking her to be his girlfriend since the third grade.

And then it happened.

GLENDALE SERIES

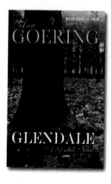  

The Glendale Series wrestles with the age-old dilemmas of love, faith, family, forgiveness and growing up in a fresh story format. With relationships that grip readers' hearts as they reflect raw realities plentiful in our society and an ending that will keep readers on the edge of their seats right up until the end, The Glendale Series is one girl's unforgettable journey to health, wholeness and joy.

MOTHERS OF GLENDALE

The Mothers of Glendale Series tells the personal, emotional, and sometimes painful stories of three special women introduced in The Glendale Series. Glendale mother figures Jari, Carla, and Hannah are each on their own journey, with their paths weaving together with one another to create a beautiful tapestry of faith, hope, and unconditional love. With raw realities that women face every day, covered by the grace of a very big God, Mothers of Glendale takes readers a step further than new love to the weathered and deeply beautiful land of seasoned marriages, motherhood and saying goodbye to a full life, well-lived.